T0157317

PRAISE FOR *THRONE OF DARKNESS*

"The meticulous detailing of the early 13th-century setting is only one of the pleasures of this series (after *Something Red* and *The Wicked*) that mixes historical fiction and horror."

—*Library Journal*

"A metropolitan collection of fascinating historical fiction . . . ever more complex with its liberal dose of magic and mysticism."

—*Booklist*

"Series newcomers will quickly feel right at home, and returning readers will enjoy learning more about their favorite characters."

—*Publishers Weekly*

"This series keeps getting better and better. . . . This is by far my favorite medieval historical series!"

—Carol Goodman, bestselling author of *The Blythewood Tales* and *The Lake of Dead Languages*

"*Throne of Darkness* takes you directly to thirteenth-century England and sticks you there until the story is done with you. . . . What Nicholas gives us is the Middle Ages in all of its fantastic weirdness and characters that belong there, serving a story that's well worth reading."

—Greg Keyes, *New York Times* bestselling author of the Kingdoms of Thorn and Bone series

PRAISE FOR *THE WICKED*

"Part mystery, part history, all spooky. . . . Read this with a well-oiled sword at hand."

—Christopher Buehlman, author of *Between Two Fires*

"An almost Dickensian level of detail transports readers to medieval England in poet Nicholas's gorgeously written novel."

—*Library Journal*

"Marvelously descriptive . . . like a more profound Harry Potter for adults."

—*Kirkus Reviews*

"*The Wicked* is the rare sequel that surpasses its predecessor."

—*Geek Library*

"Superb storytelling."

—SFGate.com

PRAISE FOR *SOMETHING RED*

One of *Kirkus Reviews'* 100 Best Novels of 2012

"A hauntingly affecting historical novel with a touch of magic."

—*Kirkus Reviews* (starred review)

"Rich in historical detail, this suspenseful coming-of-age fantasy grabs the reader with the facts of life in medieval England and the magic spells woven into its landscape."

—*Publishers Weekly* (starred review)

"This darkly atmospheric debut novel is well worth its measured plot-building for its horrific, unexpected ending."

—*Library Journal* (starred review)

"This first novel is a beauty."

—Cecelia Holland, *New York Times*
bestselling author of *The King's Witch*

"Not for the faint of heart, this pulse-pounding page-turner grabs you from the start and never lets you go. A wickedly clever and evocative combination of history, horror, mystery, and magic."

—*Booklist*

"Nicholas goes for the throat with *Something Red*. Rich in history, ankle deep in blood, and packed with brilliant writing and whip-smart plotting."

—Jonathan Maberry, *New York Times* bestselling author of *Flesh & Bone*

"Ably conjuring the beauties and drawbacks of the past, and with an engaging and unusual cast list, *Something Red* is a thoroughbred novel of nightmare terror, ruled by a force of sheer evil that seems, and may well prove, unstoppable. A *Book of Shadows* with a genuinely beating heart."

—Tanith Lee, award-winning author of *The Silver Metal Lover*

"Nicholas's beautiful prose, his detailed portrayal of life in medieval England, interesting characters, and underlying supernatural themes make this book a real gem."

—*BookBrowse*

ALSO BY DOUGLAS NICHOLAS

Throne of Darkness

The Wicked

The Demon (A Novella)

Something Red

Iron Rose

The Old Language

The Rescue Artist

In the Long-Cold Forges of the Earth

THREE QUEENS IN ERIN

A Novel

Douglas Nicholas

EMILY BESTLER BOOKS

ATRIA

New York London Toronto Sydney New Delhi

An Imprint of Simon & Schuster, Inc.
1230 Avenue of the Americas
New York, NY 10020

First Emily Bestler Books/Atria Paperback edition March 2017

EMILY BESTLER BOOKS / ATRIA PAPERBACK and colophons are trademarks of Simon & Schuster, Inc.

For information about special discounts for bulk purchases, please contact Simon & Schuster Special Sales at 1-866-506-1949 or business@simonandschuster.com

The Simon & Schuster Speakers Bureau can bring authors to your live event. For more information or to book an event, contact the Simon & Schuster Speakers Bureau at 1-866-248-3049 or visit our website at www.simonspeakers.com.

Manufactured in the United States of America

10 9 8 7 6 5 4 3 2 1

Library of Congress Cataloging-in-Publication Data is available.

ISBN 978-1-4767-5601-1
ISBN 978-1-4767-5603-5 (ebook)

for Theresa

A note on the pronunciation of Irish names:

Maeve = MAYV

Nemain = NEV-an

Aednat = AY-nith

Bradan = BRAY-dawn

Ciannait = KIN-nat

Cionnaola = KIN-ao-la

Daire = DYE-ruh

Diarmuid = DEAR-mwidge

Ferelith = FEH-reh-leeth

Fiadh = FEE-ah

Fionnuala = fin-OO-la

Macha = MACH-ah [CH as in "loch"]

Macha Mong Ruadh = MACH-ah MUNG ROO-ah

Malmhìn = MAL-veen

Nathaira = na-THAH-ra

Ó Cearbhaill = OH KYAR-oo-will

Uí Bháis = EE VAWSH

A glossary of Irish terms is to be found on page 275.

A glossary of archaisms and dialect terms is to be found on page 279.

THREE QUEENS IN ERIN

Part I

THE MAIDEN

Turn away thine eyes from me, for they have overcome me.

—Song of Solomon 6:5

Chapter 1

"Hob, *a rún*, have a wee sip of this."

Hob turned from the broad wooden rail and the sight of the horizon rising and falling, rising and falling. He took the cup from Nemain and sipped gingerly at the decoction. Immediately the mild nausea that had threatened to turn to seasickness began to subside. In the warmth that spread through his middle he recognized the base of *uisce beatha* with which Molly began so many of her remedies, augmented with a mixture of simmered herbs and spices, pleasing and pungent and so complex that he could not identify any single ingredient.

Beyond his wife, holding fast to the rail and eagerly scanning the view, was their daughter, Macha Redmane. At six years of age, she had very little fear of anything, an intense curiosity about everything, and the digestive powers of a wolf—nothing upset her stomach, not even these choppy waves of the Irish Sea. Like her mother, she wore a voluminous traveling cloak; like her mother, she had thrown back the hood thereof; like her mother, her flame-red hair streamed back in the sea wind. A well-named child, he thought, not for the first time, though she'd been named for Macha Mong Ruadh—Macha Red Mane—the only woman high king of Ireland. She imitated Nemain in everything, and Hob's life circled the two as a moth circles a lantern.

The waves were ridged with white foam, their sides veined with it. A rogue wave came in upon them slantwise; a sheet of water smacked up into the air and drenched the deck, the *boom* of its impact echoing through the hold below and setting up a chorus of bellowing and neighing from the animals penned down there. Nemain contemplated the cup in his hands, now half seawater.

"Come out of this; come under the aftercastle," she said to Hob, taking Macha's hand and tugging her from the rail.

"But, Mama, what is that, away there, do you see?" said the child, her attention on the northern horizon. They had been speaking in Irish, in which tongue Hob had attained a working facility, and now from the crow's nest came a call in English: "Sail! Two sail!"

Instantly there was a bustle from belowdecks, and a series of stentorian commands from aft, where the captain stood with the steersmen working to control the rudder. Barefoot seamen boiled out of the hatch and onto the deck;

the soles of their feet, hard as leather from going unshod and from soaking in brine, made a muffled clatter against the wood.

Hob shadowed his eyes with a broad hand and looked out to where the Irish Sea met the sky. There, two long dark shapes drove westward in parallel with their own progress, and even as he looked they altered their appearance, coming round to a course that would intercept *la Gracedieux,* the cog in which he and his family rode. The ships had a lean wolflike appearance; as they grew nearer Hob could see the high prows and sternposts that gave them an air of sea-serpent menace, the triskelion symbols worked in red twine upon their broad sails. There were six oars to a side, but these were now shipped, since the full-bellied sails were propelling them at a good clip, faster than the heavily laden *Gracedieux* could move. Clustered along the sides were helmeted men; Hob could see the glint of weapons held at the ready.

Nemain hustled her daughter under the aftercastle and down the hatchway to the hold. A moment later she was back with two bows and two quivers of arrows. Molly, her grandmother, was descending the ladder from the aftercastle deck, followed closely by her lover, Jack Brown. A moment passed while Molly assessed the situation, looking from the rapidly closing ships to the bosun passing out short broad-bladed swords and iron-headed clubs to the crew, and then she began to deploy her little family.

"'Twill be better for us to shoot from above," she said to Nemain. "Jack, Hob, arm yourselves. Jack to stand here and guard the hatch; let no one of these pirate swine who comes within your reach remain alive. Hob, range the deck and help the crew where it's help that's needed." She looked out at the two ships: birlinns, the larger, broader descendants of the Norse dragonboats. "Manxmen, by the look of them," she muttered; she spun on her heel and jumped onto the ladder, climbing rapidly upward at a pace surprising for such a large woman, and she well past her half-century mark. Nemain, ever lithe, was right behind her.

Jack threw himself at the hatchway and slid down the ladder, agile as an ape; in a moment he emerged again, tossing his crow-beak war hammer ahead of him onto the deck with a banging clatter, clambering out of the hatch with Hob's scabbarded longsword in his other hand. A burly man perhaps eight years Molly's junior, Jack was an experienced man-at-arms, a mercenary at times, a sometime Crusader, and something stranger as well.

Now he closed the hatch and stood in front of it, just beneath the overhang of the aftercastle. Hob took his sword and drew it; he tossed the scabbard behind the hatch coaming. The bosun and his assistants were back with armfuls of targes, small round shields with a spike in the center, and Hob and Jack each took one, slipping forearms through the first targe-back bracket and gripping the second.

There were two Irish merchants on board, Adam and Murchad, uncle and nephew: Adam a man in his forties, his nephew perhaps two decades younger. They imported silk, iron, and wine to Dublin, and brought away wool and hides from the interior of Ireland. They were soft unwarlike men, and now crouched down by the rail near Jack, in hope of protection by the burly man-at-arms. Each clutched a long knife, but appeared to Hob as though they would have little skill at wielding a weapon.

The birlinns were close enough now that Hob could see the men lined up at the near rails; at prow and stern were handfuls of men with grappling hooks attached to ropes, the excess in coils at their feet. There were also capstans: two forward and two aft, with the capstan bars shipped and a man at each bar. If any grapnel caught and held, the line would be bent onto the capstan and tension put on the rope, drawing the two ships together.

The birlinns began to separate. One began an attempt to cross behind the cog's stern, so to come up on the lee side; thus the two pirate crews could board simultaneously from both sides. The captain bellowed orders; seamen hauled at the ropes that altered the mainsail, and the steersmen wrestled the wheel around. The cog came about to starboard and drove between the two attackers, then veered to larboard. The three ships passed one another with archers, including Molly and Nemain, shooting at targets as they presented themselves. The two attackers now were placed on the lee side of the cog, and had to redirect their attack.

The three ships now sailed westward parallel to one another. The farther birlinn took in sail and ran out its oars, dropping behind and pulling north to regain the weather side of the cog. This left the first pirate ship running on a converging course with the cog, not far from her larboard side, and the second struggling to cross behind *la Gra-*

cedieux's stern. The first ship now ran out its oars as well in an attempt to close the distance to its prey.

There was little hope of outrunning the pirates' swift and lightly loaded craft, and the captain, apparently deciding that it was best to deal with first one and then the other rather than both at once, ordered the cog to larboard, turning toward the foe. The unexpected maneuver brought the two ships together before the pirate could ship oars, and the heavy hull of the cog snapped oars all along the birlinn's starboard side. From within the pirate vessel arose a brief but distressing chorus of shouts and screams, as the flailing inboard ends of the oars broke ribs and battered skulls.

Those pirates not needed at the oars had been clustered at their starboard rail, and some of these were clubbed down by the thrashing oars and others felled by flying splinters the length of a man's hand and the thickness of a man's thumb. Those left standing roared war cries and clashed axes against shields. Their numbers were quickly augmented by the uninjured portside rowers, and as the two ships wallowed side by side, they prepared to board.

Hob was standing amid a loose line of armed sailors, close to the larboard rail, when a flying chunk of metal whipped past his head and was immediately jerked back on a line, tearing open the shoulder of the seaman next to him and snagging onto the rail: a grapnel, a three-pronged heavy hook attached to a sturdy rope.

Now a storm of whirling grapnels broke over the deck, a blizzard of ropes, most of the hooks catching in the rail with a *chunk,* their lines quickly belayed about pins on the pirate ship or wrapped to a capstan and tightened by crewmen working the bars, the pawls clacking, the ship inexorably drawn near to the helpless cog. As the slack was taken up, the thick tarred ropes became hard as iron with the tension of holding the two heaving vessels together.

Every sailor who could be spared from working the ship now was massed at the rail, preparing to repel boarders; some had small axes and hacked at the grapnel ropes, protected by their shipmates, who contrived to cover the axmen from the pirates' arrows, angling their targes to meet the incoming shafts. The axes were not making sufficient progress: one rope parted with a crack as the strain was abruptly released, the free end lashing back toward the birlinn and striking down two of the pirates clustered at the rail, waiting to board. But the other grapnels held, even as two more flew over the rail and were drawn back to snag on the yardarm and to tangle in the rigging.

Those ropes not bent onto the capstans to bind the ships together were left to hang down the cog's side as scaling aids. And now there arose from the pirate crew another loud battle cry, heralding the rush to scramble up the cog's side. The *Gracedieux*'s crew hurled abuse and baulks of wood down on the reavers as they climbed, acrobatic as macaques, clinging to the ropes, with knives and boarding axes and the heavy cutlasses favored by seamen slung to their belts.

The cog had a small galley in the forecastle, a circle of flat stones on a bed of sand, and when the coast-hugging cog put in each night to some baylet or quiet cove, a small fire was built to heat the crew's meal. The cook had evidently kindled a small fire, sufficient to light torches from, for here he came with two of his assistants, staggering from the galley with a cauldron of poppy oil and suet, the kitchen boy following with a blazing torch in each hand. The galley gang heaved the mixture over the side onto the low-slung birlinn deck, drenching the lower corner of the pirate ship's sail. Thereupon the kitchen boy tossed the torch into the greasy pool, and a roar of flame shot up and caught the bottom of the sail, and a great cry went up from the birlinn's aftercastle, where the master and mates began to bellow orders for buckets to be lowered and to those of the crew not actually in the assault party to contain the fire, every seaman's nightmare.

And indeed there were curses and imprecations from the cog's aftercastle as the captain saw the danger to his own ship that the cook's action posed: the pirate ship's sail was already aflame and the foredeck was beginning to catch here and there. The order was given to cut loose at any cost. The seamen hacking at the ropes were forced back from their task by the boarders swarming over the rail.

A line of grappling, cursing men swiftly formed just inboard of the rail, as sailor and pirate struggled to kill one another with dagger and short cutlass, in some cases mixing wrestling holds with stabbing and cutting. In a short time men from both groups were down in their own blood.

Hob dropped his targe to the deck and with his left hand drew the war dagger Sir Balthasar had given him. Now deadly with either hand, he began a charge: from the break of the aftercastle he trotted forward just behind the line of battle, attacking any boarder who broke through the line of sailors. The pirates were Manxmen, big strongly made men: Norse-Gaels, the descendants of the Vikings who mixed with Scots of the Western Isles. But Hob was himself tall, and under Jack's tutelage he had become brawny, and under Sir Balthasar's instruction he had acquired the martial skills of the Norman knight from one of the great killers of the North Country, and from Molly and Nemain he had learned many little-known sleights and artful movements. There were now few who might best him: Sir Balthasar; perhaps Jack; and his little wife, Nemain, no match for him in strength but so deadly in her reptile speed and falcon eye that not a blow could be dealt her. Molly, of course—one never quite knew what that queenly woman was capable of, but she had lived a long time in a perilous world.

Now he ran at two pirates, axmen, and they set themselves to meet him. They wore vests of woven rope, light enough and easy enough to jettison that if a pirate fell overboard he would not be drowned as he would if he wore mail. The one on his right was slightly in advance of the other, and as the man brought his targe before him to protect his body Hob dipped and struck beneath the little shield, cutting the man's right leg so severely that he crashed to the deck, dropping his ax and clutching his thigh in an attempt to slow the torrent of blood.

The danger in assailing two such warriors at once is that in dealing with the first, one must neglect the second. Now the pirate's comrade swung a mighty overhand blow at where Hob's head would have been had he straightened, but Hob had leaped backward as he rose, anticipating just such a strike, and the ax hissed through empty air and stuck fast in the deck planking. The Manxman wasted no time in trying to free it, but ripped a sax from a sheath on his belt. He threw up the long knife in an attempt to block Hob's sword, but Hob beat it aside, and with a circling flirt of the longsword lined the blade up and thrust it into the pirate's throat. The Manxman swung the sax about erratically for a few brief moments, and then collapsed beside his shipmate.

Hob continued forward at a fast jog. He killed three men in succession, jumping each corpse and continuing to his next victim. He ran hard at a trio who had just broken the sailors' line and had turned to attack the defenders from the rear. Hob sped along behind them; even as they became aware of him he slashed left-handed with the dagger at the first, skipped the second, and hewed right-handed at the third man's neck. Few survived a full stroke to the throat with a longsword, and this man was no exception.

Hob stopped as quickly as he could; his thin leather boots slid on the planks, slippery with a mixture of seawater and the blood now beginning to overspread the deck. He was turning as he skated to a halt. At a glance he saw that the third man was dying and the first was down on one knee, gasping in pain, one hand to the back of the neck, blood sheeting down from the deep cut Hob had made with the heavy war dagger.

Hob swung a powerful blow at the remaining Manxman. The pirate tried to block it with the targe but he miscalculated. Hob's sword swept in and caught him in the ribs. To Hob's surprise the rope armor proved effective: the sword sliced the ropes but failed to cut completely through. The force of the blow was transferred to the Manxman's body, though, and he crabbed over with the pain in his ribs. Realizing his peril, he tried to straighten and back away and aim a blow with his ax; Hob caught the axhead on the quillons of his dagger and closed with the pirate. At so close a distance, the longsword was ineffective as an edged weapon: Hob smashed the side of his adversary's skull with the sword's heavy iron pommel, disengaged the dagger from the axhead, and thrust it up under the rope-vest armor. The thick knife-blade did appalling things to the pirate's inwards; the man's eyes rolled upward and he fell away from Hob.

A sudden bulk loomed at the edge of his vision. Hob sprang sideways, but he was off balance, staggering toward his right, and now he could see the pirate, a short heavy cutlass held over his head in both hands, aiming to cleave Hob's head in two. He brought the war dagger around to block it—the sword was far out of position—but even the dagger was too late, too late. He tensed for the blow.

A black-feathered arrow pierced the bandit's armpit, just above where the rope vest began, and he screamed and dropped the cutlass clanging to the deck. A moment later he sat down heavily and began to pull feebly at the projecting staff. But there are conduits beneath the arm that channel the all-important blood; once these are interfered with, life drifts away. The victim is outwardly almost unmarked; within, all is chaos.

Hob looked toward the aftercastle; Molly stood there,

sending shafts along the cog's deck, striking down boarders; it was she who had saved him. Nemain, standing a little aft of Molly, shot down and forward, onto the birlinn's deck and the pirates there attempting to quench the fire. He ran lightly back along the deck to kill any who opposed him, but between the fire on the pirate vessel and the resistance of the cog's crew, there were only two brigands left, and he dealt with them swiftly.

He became aware that *la Gracedieux*'s captain was roaring at his crew to cut the burning birlinn loose before their own sail caught. The tarred ropes on the pirate vessel now were lines of fire from the deck to the yard from which hung the broad sail. The symbol on the sail, three conjoined armored legs within a circle, was enveloped in a sheet of flame, and the bottom half of the sail was already blackened, shredded to smoking ribbons that fluttered and detached, hissing as they fell into the waves.

There came a mighty whistle. He looked around. Jack was beckoning him urgently. He jogged over. The dark man pointed to the hatchway, then to Hob; he indicated himself, then mimed cutting the ropes. Hob nodded, and took up guard over the hatchway. Jack dropped his hammer beside the hatch and ran to the rail. He took axes from two of the Manx corpses and, shoving crewmen aside, began to chop at the first binding rope, left-right left-right, tremendous blows that no one could match. Jack's strength was unparalleled in Hob's experience, and in short order the rope parted with a *bang!* and whipped back onto the brigands' ship. Jack moved down the rail, severing rope after rope, and in a short while the cog was free, moving away from the birlinn, which, with its sail burnt and half its oars smashed, was crippled in the water, its crew trying to save itself from being burned to death, or drowned in the pitiless swells of the Irish Sea.

Chapter 2

All along the deck of the cog lay corpses: crewmen and pirates, stretched in pools of their own blood. The surviving crew, much reduced, began heaving the Manx bodies overboard near the bows and laying their fallen comrades to one side for Christian burial in Dublin. When Jack returned to the hatchway, Hob retrieved his scabbard from where he'd tossed it and sheathed his sword. He thrust the scabbard through his belt at the back and trotted up to help clear the deck of its dead.

He and a handful of other sailors dragged body after body to the rail, leaving smeared indistinct trails of red across the deck planking. A chanted count, a grunting lift, and a splash; then back for another one.

Those sailors not engaged in this work were trying to clear the tangle of cut ropes from the deck and reset the sail; the captain was calling orders from the aftercastle. He was still trying to outmaneuver the second birlinn, which despite his best efforts was closing in on his starboard side.

Hob had his hand hooked in a dead pirate's belt, and a crewman on the other side of the corpse was calling "and one, and two, and—" when he heard the *clank* and *crunch* of grapnels biting into the wood of the rail. Over the corpse went, and Hob spun about to see what was toward.

Beside the after quarter of the cog loomed the bows of the second birlinn. Three of the grapnels had metal prongs stuck deep in the ship's wood, and as he watched, two more whirled through the air. One bounced on the deck but failed to gain purchase as it was pulled back; it slid over the rail and out of sight. The other one caught and held, and the rope was yanked tight.

A moment later a mob of yelling men poured over the rail, their boarding axes and short stout-bladed cutlasses hacking into the crewmen attempting to repel the attack. Sailors dropped ropes and seized weapons and sprang to the ship's defense, and for a moment the pirates were driven back a few paces. A clanging as of many smiths at a forge arose as blades clashed against one another, and then the relentless reinforcement of the pirate force, as more and more men vaulted the railing, began to tell. Seamen were cut down where they stood or killed as they turned to flee, and in a few heartbeats thirty or forty men claimed possession of the after half of the deck.

Molly and Nemain had perhaps six arrows left between them. Nothing but Jack Brown separated the pirate mob from the hatch beneath which was Hob and Nemain's daughter, or the ladder that led up to where Nemain and Molly stood. Few men, it was true, could face Jack and his hammer, but even that powerful man could be overwhelmed by nigh on two score men.

Even as Hob took stock of how matters stood, Molly killed a man with an arrow dead center in his chest. The pirate crashed to the deck, and writhed a moment, then lay still. As one, the pirates turned their eyes to the aftercastle: the two women with their bows standing near the lip of the upper deck, the captain and two sailors wrestling the wheel about, trying to break the cog free of the constricting grapnel ropes, and, lurking beneath the aftercastle, the broad-shouldered form of Jack Brown, a targe on his left arm and his crow-beak hammer in his right hand.

A pirate broke into the high-pitched battle cry of the Manxmen, inciting a concerted rush aft. Jack's hammer swung in a gleaming arc, the beak sinking into one attacker's neck and immediately withdrawn, the backswing smashing another Manxman's skull.

Hob pulled his scabbard from his belt, out from behind his back, and ripped the sword from its sheath. He started down the deck, reaching across his body and drawing his war dagger crosswise. He broke into a run, shouting, "*Ban-ríon Maeve abú!*" A few of the pirates closest to him turned about and braced themselves for his onslaught. He whirled the sword high and struck the nearest pirate down, his neck half-severed; with the dagger he punched into the midsection of another.

Now for a moment he was the center of a storm of counterstrokes from those brigands closest to him, and he was forced to parry at a furious rate, plying dagger and sword in swift alternation. His blood began to heat up, and his fears for his dear ones, on the far side of this crowd of men, began to transmute into rage at these intruders into his life, threatening his family in the course of preying upon others for gain.

It was a dangerous place to be, between Hob and his loved ones. The pirates were Norse Gaels, who tended to be big men, but Hob was a tall man, and strong, and he had been taught weaponry by masters, and he was working himself into a battle fury. Steel flicked past his face, but he had leaned back just enough, and now he lunged, struck through a pirate's rope armor to his heart, and sprang back; he caught a thrust on his dagger, turned it aside, and slid the dagger-blade up till it locked on the quillons of the pirate's cutlass, and bashed the man in the face with his sword's pommel. Almost immediately he parried strokes from right and left simultaneously with his long and short steel.

He began to move as though he and his opponents were in a dance in which only he knew the steps. Time slowed and, insofar as he was thinking at all, he thought that he almost knew what would happen before it did happen, so attuned to his foes was he. While he dealt with the rank before him, he was feeling out ways that he might murder those in the rank behind, and he felt himself to be the only one moving at full speed—the brigands seemed very slow to him.

He cut, he thrust, he hacked; at the end of each blow

was the jolt, the thick and yielding opposition of meat to the cleaver. His sleeves were soaked with blood; the front of his shirt was sodden with gore. No sword seemed able to reach him: he whirled and leaped and sprang from side to side like one possessed by hell-devils, and every bound that he made ended in wounding or death for the Manxmen.

They began to fear him. Except for those closely engaged with Jack, the mass of the pirates had turned to face Hob, pressing forward to deal with this unexpected threat from their rear. But now the men immediately facing him began to step left and right to avoid engaging him, hoping that he would storm past them, and perhaps be killed by others. As they cringed back to either side of the deck, pressing against the rails, black-fletched arrows from the women aloft on the afterdeck took their toll of the stationary targets they presented.

An opening appeared before Hob. He stepped into it and then, hardly knowing why, by pure instinct jumped back abruptly, a prodigious leap. The pirates to either side of the space slashed with ax and cutlass at where he should have been. The cutlass whistled through empty air, but the axman buried his weapon by mischance in his comrade's skull. As he stood gaping at what he had done, Hob cut him down.

He killed his way down the deck, hacking, hacking, and on under the afterdeck. It was shadowed here, and there was a real or imagined red mist before his eyes. A pirate seemed to kneel in abrupt surrender, but then Hob realized that the man was dead on his knees, and Jack was putting a foot to the corpse's shoulders to tug his hammer's crow-beak free.

There were two men left by the rail and Hob whirled to take them; his sword swung up and hovered an instant before the downstrike. Then:

"Jesus and Mary, don't kill us!" cried Adam, he and his nephew hunkered in a crouch, arms bent and held before their faces in a futile attempt to block the threatened blow. Hob knew them and did not know them; he fought for sanity as his body yearned toward murder; his arm wanted to fall and rise and fall again, to add two more bodies to those strewn across the deck behind him. He stood, red from head to thigh, the whites of his eyes staring out from a face painted crimson with the hearts' blood of his enemies. "Sure it looked like Satan come to collect souls," was how Murchad described it, safe in a tavern two nights later.

"Hob! Give over, give over, *a rún*!" It was Nemain's voice, sharp as a snapping stick, calling in English the better to reach him through whatever possessed him. Hob stood a very long moment, then stepped back and looked around. His wife clung with one hand to the ladder up to the aftercastle, a reddened dagger in one hand—apparently at some point the fighting had come to close quarters with her as well. "'Tis done, husband, 'tis done." Jack was standing looking at him; Molly was beginning to descend the ladder; the Irish merchants were frozen in place. Except for some sailors up by the bows, everyone else on this level was dead.

When the captain, Master Hugh of Portsmouth, had managed to set *la Gracedieux* on course again, the ship limping toward Dublin harbor, and Molly and Nemain had bound up what wounds there were among the crew still left alive, there was a small gathering under the aftercastle, where the captain had, not exactly a cabin, but a sheltered cubby he could retreat to, with a cot and a rudimentary table, for those nights he spent aboard when the ship was docked at some port of call. The merchants had donated a barrel of wine, and the crew had been issued a double ration, and now Molly and her troupe, the merchants, and the captain sat on bench and crate, crowded into the captain's lair.

"To Mistress Molly and her family, without whom I trow we'd all be slaves or dead," said Master Hugh.

"'Twas a blessing they were aboard," said Murchad.

"Aye," said his uncle, "though I was thinking that this gentleman was the Angel of Death, and I was afraid he wasn't going to be contented with just those pirates. May I ask your name, sir?"

At a quick dark glance from Nemain, Hob stopped himself from saying "Sir Robert," for so he thought of himself now, and said only, "I am called Robert."

"You're English, surely, and it's well-spoken you are, sir. Are you Norman, then?" asked Uncle Adam.

Hob, an orphan of whose parents nothing was known but that they were dead, thought, not for the first time, well, I *may* in fact be Norman, but I'll never know. Aloud he said, "No, I'm just an Englishman like our captain here, and"—nodding to Molly and the others—"we are traveling people."

"Well, Robert the Englishman, 'tis glad we are of your company, and God and Mary be with you and your family here, and they defending us as well. But—by Our Lady!—I've never seen so much killing by one man in so short a time. I'm no warrior, but I've been in merchant caravans that were attacked, and 'twas not like this atall. This . . . 'twas like a wolf in a pen of sheep."

Molly had once had a vision, as she did now and then, of the future, and she had said then, "Be said by me, one day kerns will call you Robert the Englishman. . . . Foemen will step away to the right hand and the left, fearing to engage you, the dread champion in Erin."

Now she raised her cup. She looked around, then straight at Hob, and said, slowly and distinctly, "To Robert the Englishman."

A significant look passed around Molly's troupe. Nemain and Jack raised their cups, and they drank to Hob, and he in turn proposed a health: "To our arrival in Erin!"

Of course the English captain and the Irish merchants drank to their commercial destination, but Molly's troupe had in their thoughts as well a journey toward bloodletting, toward revenge, toward the recovery of their heritage, as the ship wallowed under shortened sail through the waning afternoon, over the darkening seas, toward Ireland and their destiny.

Chapter 3

OFTEN A DAM THAT HAS STOOD for years, with nothing but the occasional small leak to show the wear of time and water, will, following a spring thaw or a powerful storm, give way all at once, the fitted blocks of stone tumbling downward and outward and the white-foaming water rushing through as though in a frenzy of joy at its new freedom. Yet the day before, all seemed solid and immovable.

So it came about that last year, back in England, on a chill October evening, Samhain still a week away, with its gifts for the dead to be left out the night before, Molly's reserve about the past gave way—under what pressures Hob could only guess—and she began at last to speak of the disaster that had befallen her clan. Before this she had spoken only in the most general terms: an attack by a clan of strangers, wanderers outlawed in their homeland who were looking to find a foothold on Erin's wild western coast; Nemain's parents slain, the clan scattered, and Molly fleeing with her granddaughter to England, to anonymity, to safety. Partly it was to spare Nemain distress; partly it was to conceal all ties to Erin, lest assassins spy them out; partly it was too painful for Molly herself to dwell upon.

On this night, camped at the edge of a wood in the west of England, not far from the shore of the Irish Sea, the four adults—accompanied, of course, by Sweetlove, who was to be found wherever Jack was—were talking quietly prior to retiring. A cold rain was drumming on the roof of Molly's big wagon. Dinner had been eaten and Jack had pulled down Molly's big bed, and Macha Redmane was already tucked in and deeply asleep. Except when Molly was entertaining Jack, the child slept with her great-grandmother, which left Hob and Nemain the privacy of the middle wagon, while Jack and Sweetlove claimed the small wagon.

Tonight Hob was half sitting, half reclining on the side of the bed not taken up by Redmane, who had a little queen's tendency to sprawl and claim her territory. Hob had his back to the wall with Nemain lying against his chest, wrapped in his arms, and Molly, who had been unusually quiet all day, brought forth a jug of the *uisce beatha* and poured for everyone.

Jack was sitting on a storage chest that served as a bench, redoubled woolen blankets atop it providing a comfortable seat, and Molly now sat down beside him, cup in hand, and leaned against the soldier's arm. She was a large woman, but

Jack, powerful Jack, might have been a wall for all the effect her weight had on him. After a moment he moved his arm to hold her about her waist, and she shifted into a more comfortable position. Sweetlove, dozing on Jack's lap, stirred and grumbled a bit but did not wake.

The two couples sat quietly for a time, echoing one another in their positions, until Molly took another drink, cleared her throat, and spoke.

"I'm thinking that now, with both the Church and a fine group of knights being allies as they are, 'tis perhaps time we spoke, we four, of our future, in clear terms. 'Tis well to draw the bow, and to draw it full back to the ear, but the moment comes when one must let the arrow fly, and that moment is close at hand.

"And if we are to speak of the future in Erin, it's first that I must speak of the past in Erin, though my heart aches to think of it."

Hob was intensely interested: he had never heard the full story of how Molly and Nemain had come to be cast up on England's shores. The women had indicated that they did not wish to dwell on it, and Hob was too careful of their wishes to insist.

Molly gazed a moment at the opposite wall of the wagon, her eyes with the unfocused stare of one who looks into the past, and then began.

"I had decided to take Nemain to meet the *Bean na beacha*, the Woman of the Bees. Sometimes we just call her the Beekeeper. No one remembers her true name. She is one of the greatest practitioners of the Art in Erin. No one knows how old she is, but she is very old. She has a glen in the West of Erin, and no one may enter that glen if she does not permit them. She dwells there alone save for her bees, her goats, her dog, and every creature of the woodland: none of them fear her, nor does she fear wolf or bear. To look at her, she is a wee old woman, if sprightly, but she has the Crone power to a greater degree than any living woman."

Hob did not like to interrupt, but he did not want to misunderstand in a matter that might involve their survival.

They were speaking in English for Jack's benefit—Hob could limp along in Irish but Jack had no head for it. Now Hob asked, "Crone power, *seanmháthair*? What might that be?"

Since his marriage to Nemain, since his becoming a knight as well as a father-to-be, it seemed to the women inappropriate for him to address Molly as "Mistress," and he had, with some discomfort, changed to "grandmother" in Irish, although she was actually his liege as well, he having sworn his knighthood to her in her capacity as queen.

Molly looked at Nemain for a moment, as if asking where to begin with all this. Her granddaughter just nodded encouragingly, and patted Hob's arm. "He's a clever enough husband, most of the time," she said. "Just tell him about the Mothers, and go on from there."

Molly cleared her throat. "I'm not wanting to burden you with this before, *a rún*, you a Christian as you are and our Art being a trouble to your mind, but this is something you must know, for it tells you somewhat of our enemies as well. Is it that you remember me telling that Berber priest, Father . . . Father . . ."

"Ugwistan," said Hob.

"The very same. And myself telling him somewhat of the Mórrígan, how she was three queens and one queen at the same time, and he thinking of your Trinity, and that papal agent da Panzano pulling him up sharp. I took a liking to Father Ugwistan, so I did; he was a man you could speak with and he listening and not turning away in scorn."

Hob nodded. "I liked him as well. He did not seem so, well, sour and disapproving as Monsignor da Panzano."

"Ah, well—the Mórrígan is not the only Power that is three-in-one. 'Tis the Mothers who encompass the powers of women; there are three, but they are also one: the Maiden, the Mother, and the Crone. The Maiden is the power of women in their youth: to walk in beauty, to move in grace, to draw men to their side. The Mother is the giver of life, the ruler of the household or the tribe. The Crone is the power of women in age: wisdom, memory of how things may best be done, and mastery of the Art. There are male masters of the Art—that Berber sorcerer Yattuy was one, and Sir Tarquin was another—but they are on different paths, as 'twere—their power does not come from the Female Mysteries. In general women are more powerful in the Art, being more alert to the world—"

"They do not go blundering through the world with their great strong bodies and thick limbs," said Nemain to her husband with a tone of sweet mockery, "like bulls trampling through a flower garden."

Hob gave her a small playful shove, but said nothing: he did not want to further delay Molly's discourse.

"—and older women of the Art are more powerful than younger," said Molly, ignoring them both, "for their understanding mounts up year by year, and this is Crone power: grandmother wit and an ever-strengthening grasp of the shadow world."

Molly nodded toward Macha, her closed and peaceful face turned to the ceiling, one arm flung out over the edge of the bed, her small perfect fingers curled lightly toward her palm. "I had said of the Mórrígan, when Father Ugwistan was trying to grasp Her nature, that She was three queens, three queens in Erin, and you, Hob, remembering this, when you found that Nemain was carrying your daughter and she to be a queen as well, and the three of us to return to Erin, lifted your drink 'to three queens in Erin.' 'Twas then that a shadow passed over my heart."

"But why, *seanmháthair*?" said Hob, sitting up slowly, gently putting Nemain aside; a happy memory for him was acquiring a sinister undertone.

"There are also three queens in Erin who are not *of* Erin. The clan of murderers and breakers of guest-oath who took our home is ruled by three queens, and they are very like the Mothers, save that they are evil where the Mothers are good. They are sisters, with nine years between the eldest and the next eldest; and another nine years before the birth of the youngest.

"That youngest, Malmhìn, perhaps five and twenty summers and unmarried still, is half an animal herself—she lives in the greenwood part of the year, and is said to catch and eat raw squirrel, and to go clothed in the skins of small animals, save when she is among other folks—then she'll wear the simplest coarsest garments, as one who is lacking in wit. She is no shapeshifter, but she has some Beast power, in that men cannot resist her. She is too much a sylvester, a wild woman of the woods, to govern the tribe.

"The middle sister, Ferelith, is weak in the Art, but is like Hob here, a thinker. She rules the clan and is not unskilled at statecraft, for her clan has usurped a part of the West of Erin by treachery and bloodshed, and yet she has been able to play the neighboring clans, even those that my people had treaties with, against one another in such a way that they do not unite against the intruders and drive them off the cliffs, into the Western Ocean. She is as well a battle queen, a woman of her hands, and her clan is a fierce one in war.

"The clan itself is tainted with evil—they are from the *Innse Gall,* the isles of the strangers, the Western Isles of Scotland, where the Northmen settled and mingled with the Scots. These people are now *Gall-Ghaedheil*—'Foreign Gaels,' the Norse Gaels who rule the Isles, like those Manx pirates—big-limbed powerful men, with the Viking skill at armor. There are whole clans who make their living by hiring out as mercenaries, and such as those we call *gallóglaigh,* foreign warriors."

"In English 'tis 'gallowglasses,' *seanmháthair,*" said Nemain.

"Gallowglasses, aye, and every one of them with a mail

coat to his knee, and an ax that's five feet in length. Our Irish clansmen fight in their linen shirts, scorning armor, and sure it's done them no benefit against armored Norman or armored gallowglass. These men of the Scottish Isles present a wall of knitted iron, and their terrible axes licking out from that wall. The men of the tribe are not herdsmen and warriors, or farmers and warriors, or craftsmen and warriors, as are the Ó Cearbhaills: they are professional warriors—that is, 'tis fighting that they sell, and their services go to kings and lords who can pay for them, and for meat and drink they have slaves or near-slaves who work their farms and tend their flocks. 'Tis war that is their very profession, and so they are like your Norman knights, and think of war all the time, and train, and in short, they are accomplished at it.

"Our men are warriors to protect their people, and let me be honest, to do a little cattle-raiding now and then, but they gain their bread by other means than warfare, honest means, and have not elaborate arms nor heavy armor. They snatch a sword, a spear, and they're away onto their ponies in the clothes they're wearing: that's the Ó Cearbhaills. They are brave, they are high-spirited, but they are not well-matched with these grim iron-clad practitioners of death.

"The gallowglasses fight on foot, and they are swift on attack and slow on retreat, and sworn to scorn death when once committed to a battle, and 'tis Norman knights such as yourself, Sir Robert, and Sir Balthasar, that are needed, 'tis knights with their own mail hauberks and their long shields and their great horses that are needed to break a wall of gallowglasses, and even then 'tis uncertain who will prevail.

"This clan that have settled here like locusts on a field of grain, they are gallowglasses like the MacSweeneys or the MacDowells of the Isles, but so disliked are they, even among other gallowglass tribes, for their vile sorceries and their plundering greed and their oath-breaking that, so I am hearing on this side and that, the Lord of the Isles banished the whole clan, and set them wandering, and they surrendered whatever name they had in the Isles, and took the name *Uí Bháis*, the Tribe of Death.

"But more than the youngest daughter with her enchantments of the flesh, more than the battle queen with her gallowglass cohorts, it is the eldest that is to be feared—she has the Crone power of which I spoke, but in her it is dark and evil. Nathaira—in the language of the Scots, so like our own Irish, it means 'snake'—may not be her true name: many practitioners of the Art, and especially the dark Art, seek to conceal their true names lest they give power over them to their enemies; 'tis the same with the Beekeeper. It was by Nathaira's power that our clan was overwhelmed. 'Tis why, when you drank that health in all innocence, I felt the shadow."

"And yet your . . . Patron, the Mórrígan, is three queens in one," said Hob, with his tendency to think things through to their end, "and the, the Grandmothers . . . ?"

"The Mothers," said Nemain quietly.

"The Mothers," said Hob, "they three queens are not evil

either, are they? And yourself, *seanmháthair,* and Nemain, and now Redmane—you will be another three, and none of you evil. Well, perhaps Nemain, a bit, but—"

Here it was Nemain's turn to deliver a mock blow with her elbow against his ribs.

"—and so there is no need to think that it was these evil sisters who drew any aid from my little salute."

Molly looked at him and a slow smile spread over her face. "Did I not choose well for you, *a chuisle*?" she said to Nemain. "The thought that Hob's cup-pledge was an ill omen has been a weight—a small weight, but a weight—on my heart for years, and myself just putting it aside and not thinking of it, and here 'tis lifting from me now, just with this little bit of good sense he's speaking."

"He's a grand husband when he's not insulting me," said Nemain with a grin.

Molly took a drink, and then another. She was silent for a while, and her expression slowly grew grimmer. "Those days, those evil days! We suspected nothing—everything came down upon us, sudden as a thunderbolt, and Nemain and I one day secure and the next kinless refugees. Much of what I know about the Uí Bháis I learned later, from a scattered kinsman here and there, from the tales of travelers, even from my own use of the water mirror.

"But on a day the three queens, they're coming by themselves, poorly dressed and seeking refuge, to our hall. They tell of having to flee the slaughter of their clan, as I found myself doing a short time later. We're taking them in, the poor things, and I'm sensing no harm in them, for that's how powerful a worker of the Art the eldest sister was.

"I'd planned to take Nemain to see the Woman of the Bees, that the child might see what the fullness of the Art was like, and learn, not craft, but a sense of how the old woman lived, in harmony with the world, and with benevolence in her Art.

"And so, thinking nothing amiss, a day or so after the three queens came, we two took a pony cart, and our harps—for the old woman knew all the old songs, and I thought we'd sing with her—and we drove up into the hills, and by ways I knew came to the pass into her glen, and waited there till we were given permission to proceed."

"There were guards, then?" said Hob.

"None that one could see," said Nemain. "But there were guards—you could feel them."

"Feel them?"

"'Tis a reluctance to go farther that comes upon you," said Molly. "And soon you're sitting there, the pony as well not willing to go farther, and you feel you can go not one more English yard."

"But how are you given permission to proceed, if there's no one there?" asked Hob.

"After a time—not long, not long—a small bird, perhaps a wren, perhaps a goldcrest, flits down and perches on the cartwheel, and looks you in the eye, and sings a short song, and the . . . reluctance . . . lifts, and the bird flies off, and you whistle up the pony and jog into the Beekeeper's glen."

"'Tis a place of beauty, that glen," said Nemain, in a

voice uncharacteristically wistful for one who was usually brisk and cheerful, and sometimes sarcastic.

"She has shaped and trained it, that glen," said Molly, "planting here and weeding there: a brook wanders through carpets of wildflowers; there are strong overshadowing trees that shelter her dwelling; orchards of trees that bear fruit; there are swarms of songbirds; and under everything the hum of the bees, hive after hive. Herself has a fine cottage, the walls woven of wattle and the roof thatched—'tis not overlarge from the front, but it backs into the hillside, so that there is much more inside, to the rear, rooms cut into the living rock.

"And here is this wee white-haired woman, old enough to be my own grandmother—in truth, I cannot say how old she might be—and one of the most powerful mages I've yet to come nigh. You can feel the power coming off her like the heat from a hearthstone."

"I remember it so clearly, that feeling; I'm saying to you at the time that my bones were happy within me, and myself no older than Macha at the time," said Nemain.

"Aye," said Molly, "and the first thing the Beekeeper did was give us drink, honey beer for myself and berry-water for Nemain, for the day was warm, and the second thing she did was unhitch the pony with her own small suntanned hands, and turn it out into the meadow to graze, and drink of the stream.

"And then we sat in wicker chairs, not far from the rows of hives, and spoke of the Art. It seemed to me at first to be a quiet conversation on a drowsy afternoon, myself just intending to introduce Nemain to her and to have Nemain see this little giant of magecraft.

"After a bit, listening to her voice and feeling so comfortable that I might have lain down there amid the wildflowers and had a wee nap, I'm realizing that she's giving Nemain a lesson, all coated with a kind of honey of jests and stories about the fairy folk and such, so that the child was learning a mort of lore without realizing that she was being taught. 'Tis said that she can tell the bees what she wants and they obey, and she was no less deft with the child here.

"What's more, I'm realizing that there are things she's speaking of that myself did not know, and it's then that I'm sitting up and pricking up my ears as this one does." She pointed to Sweetlove, who, despite being curled up on Jack's lap with eyes squeezed shut, was swiveling an ear to and fro to keep track of each speaker.

Hob, looking back and forth between his wife and her grandmother, saw the same softness of expression, a dreamy faraway look, as each recalled the serenity of the Beekeeper's home, the Beekeeper's presence. And as he watched, a certain dismay crept into each countenance: their mouths turned down, their brows drew together.

"And then . . ." said Nemain.

"Aye, and then," said Molly. "In the midst of this drowsy afternoon, a wren flies to the arm of Herself's chair, and perches there, and looks at her, and makes not a sound. And a shadow comes across her features, and she says to Nemain, 'Wait here, child, and finish your cup,' and to me she says, 'Come within,' and we rose and I followed her in. I knew she'd learned that something was amiss, from that bird, though not a sound had it made.

"Now, my own grandmother had taught me the craft of the water mirror, but over the years the Beekeeper showed me uses for it that my grandmother knew nothing of. On this day she took me to one of the rooms in the back, a room dug into the rock, and in no time atall she had a basin with water set up and prayers said, and then she bade me look.

"And within the water I could see the shore by my clan's hall, and the birlinns drawn up on the strand, and companies of gallowglasses filing along the paths that led up the cliffside; and then she showed me my own hall, and Macha my daughter and Cionnaola her husband, my beloved son-in-law, and they sitting with eyes open but unable to move, and the long table with the best warriors of our clan, and they paralyzed as well. You could see them breathe, and their eyes rolling from side to side, and now and again a hand would twitch, but plainly they could not arise.

"And at the head of the table sat the younger two sisters, and the eldest was on her feet with a small brazier burning herbs, and her hand outstretched over the company, and through the water mirror I could hear, not loud but clear, her voice—such a voice! Ragged, throaty, imperious!—chanting in the Scottish tongue, words so old that though I speak the Gaelic of the Scots I could not understand them, but still, I could tell they were a spell, a spell of binding.

"And then in came the gallowglass constable—for such is what their war leader is called—and a squad of his men behind him, clad in their long mail coats and their long heavy gloves with their long single-headed axes, and their helmets that show almost nothing but their eyes, and they went up and down the table like harvesters reaping barley, and they struck the heads from everyone, even my own beautiful Macha."

"Jesus, Mary, and Joseph!" said Hob, appalled. Neither he nor Jack had heard this story except in its most vague outlines—they knew Molly's clan had been scattered and her lands usurped, and that Nemain had been orphaned, but neither Nemain nor her grandmother had ever spoken directly of it.

Molly fell silent, and she put her hand over her eyes. Even Jack, who when a mercenary had seen his share of horrors, looked distressed, perhaps for Molly's sake. He still held her about her waist, and now he stroked her shoulder. She sighed and took her hand from her face.

"I sat with the old woman for a time, she speaking wisdom into my ear and putting courage into my heart and strength into my limbs, for she is kind to the core and we had been friends a long time. She's giving me a store of silver, and some gold, and advising me to go eastward into the land of the English, and dwell there some years, and return and drive the Uí Bháis into the sea, for she saw into the time-to-come far more clearly than I, and I am no child at divining what will come. 'They will scatter your clan, for they mean to settle here; they have nowhere else to go,' she said, and so it proved.

"And then 'twas time for me to stand up, and go out to Nemain, and put it to her as gently as I could that her parents were dead and her world changed for aye. The old woman sat with us and helped, and Nemain was brave beyond my hopes, but 'twas an evil hour."

" 'Twas," said Nemain. She was not weeping, but she'd laid her face against Hob's heart, and she kept her eyes tight shut, and she clutched at his shirt.

"So we made our way across Erin to Dublin, and from thence into Wales, and I used the old woman's silver to get us this big wagon to live and travel in, and a horse, not young, that drew the wagon till it died—a sweet old horse, and didn't it lie down in a pasture one night when we'd camped and next morning it was cold.

"We were at a farmer's fair, and there was young Milo to be had, and already trained to the yoke. Nemain and I played for our supper, and later I gathered herbs and such that I knew and healed folk, and at whiles I made the *uisce beatha,* and so we maintained ourselves, and when I met Jack, I had set enough by for a second and later a third wagon.

"And all the time I was listening for word of what transpired away in the West of Erin. Such tidings are scant and far between, but much of what I know about the Uí Bháis I learned at this time, from pilgrims crossing England to go on to the Holy Land, and once or twice exiles from Erin—outlaws, wolf's heads—sick for their home and glad to talk to me in our own language."

She looked at Hob. "And one day we came by chance to the little village of Saint Edmund, and ourselves welcomed by an old priest with an orphan boy in his care. You were a handsome young lad, Hob, and I reached out and stroked your hair, and didn't I feel one of the most powerful jolts from it! I knew then, I knew to my bones that you were Nemain's man-to-be. I'd never seen anything with the second sight that was so clear to me."

She drank deeply, and looked at nothing for a bit. "And here we are," she said.

Everyone was quiet for a good long while. Hob sat with his thoughts whirling. The rain pattered on the roof and he was in the midst of his family: his beautiful and dangerous little wife; her extraordinary grandmother, a queen and priestess; the powerful and haunted Jack; Hob's beloved Macha Redmane; even that wee dog, Sweetlove, curled up and snoring in a high register. He stroked Nemain's hair and made soft soothing noises, and contemplated the confluence of so many rivulets of tragedy, running down to the village of St. Edmund's one narrow street, and sweeping him away on the river of his life, that had become a thing of beauty and wonder to him.

HOB HAD TRAVELED with Molly and her lover and her granddaughter for a year and a half without suspecting the tales that lay back in their lives: to him Molly was like the mother he had not had, and Jack, an immensely strong, mostly silent man, very like an uncle. Nemain and he soon became playmates, and indeed were much like brother and sister. It was an interesting life, for they traveled constantly, playing their music at inn and village and castle, and Molly dispensed herbs and set bones and did other such healing. Hob learned to play the symphonia, and so became another musician in a family of musicians.

Then, one terrible winter, they were hounded across the Pennines by a monstrous evil, and found themselves trapped by the snows in Sir Jehan's castle in the Pennine Mountains, Blanchefontaine. On what became known as Fox Night, Molly and Jack overcame a shapeshifter, and earned Sir Jehan's and Sir Balthasar's friendship and support.

On this night Hob learned that Jack had been bitten by a shapeshifter in the Holy Land, and had contracted the curse: he turned into a Beast at intervals, driven to eat of human flesh and drink of human blood. Molly kept this condition in check with her knowledge of remedies, of amulets, of the Old Gods of Ireland. Hob had decided to accept this, or more precisely to think of it as little as possible, despite being a Christian himself.

Sir Jehan had recommended Molly to his friend Sir Odinell, when that knight complained of an eerie and evil neighbor who had come to dwell by his castle, Chantemerle, on the coast of the German Sea. Molly had gained his support as well, for she destroyed the source of the uncanny murders that plagued Sir Odinell's people.

And, her reputation of dealing with these unusual perils having come to the attention of the somewhat sinister papal legate Monsignor Bonacorso da Panzano, she was pressed into service to counter a threat to the stability of England at the behest of the powerful Pope Innocent III, and so won Church support for her return to Ireland.

The gradual accumulation of treasure and friendship

had finally come to fruition. They had assembled a collection of powers, both clerical and secular, with an agreement to meet in the West of Ireland, where lay Molly's ancestral lands, to seek to oust the usurpers, and—not least—to avenge the murders of Molly and Nemain's kin.

Chapter 4

Creaking boards, nailed as buffers to pilings sunk deep in the Liffey's muddy bed, took the strain as *la Gracedieux* shouldered her way up to the wharf. The captain had judged the ship's momentum so strictly that the ship barely kissed the wharf, the board walls swaying inward but a little, and then the anchors fore and aft plunged down into the muck of the river bottom.

Dockworkers caught the stout cables heaved onto the dock and made them fast to iron bollards. The ship's crew was working shorthanded, because so many men had perished in the battle, and things proceeded more slowly than usual. But eventually a wide section of the decking toward the aftercastle was relieved of its thick wooden clamps and lifted free, to provide substantial access to the hold.

A long ramp was set up from the lip of the opening down to the hold; the ramp was propped beneath by timbers and had thin slats of wood nailed across its width to provide traction. A combined work crew of sailors and dockhands wrestled a second ramp, this one from deck to dock, into place.

A draw harness of ropes, fashioned with the cunning knots that only sailors know, was attached to Molly's big wagon, and a gang of twenty men, hauling on ropes with loops tied in at intervals, drew it to the deck. At this point they reversed it, and let it roll slowly down the ramp to the wharf. When the process had been repeated with the small wagon and the midsized wagon, Hob went down to the malodorous stalls where the draft animals were penned. Their fear at the strange circumstances, the dimness, the unstable footing as the deck shifted to the movement of the waters, was apparent in the way they stood shivering and rolling their eyes. Milo the ox gave a bleat as he saw Hob making his way down the central passageway between stalls.

"Hush now, hush now," said Hob, shoving at the ox's big shoulder to gain access to the rope by which Milo was tethered. He pushed the ox backward and eventually got him out into the passage. He led the beast aft to the beginning of the ramp; at this point Milo registered his disapproval of yet one more indignity by the simple expedient of stopping abruptly, all twelve hundredweight rendered as immobile as a boulder.

Hob turned and put his arm across the ox's powerful neck. He stroked him under the jaw and murmured in his ear, "There now, Lambkin, 'tis not so terrible; there's a nice ramp to walk up and another down and there you'll be on wonderful solid land again, and there's grass to eat, and . . ." and much more of this nonsense in the soothing voice he used to send Redmane to sleep. A couple of the English sailors were standing by, arms crossed, and grinning—but behind their hands: they had seen Robert the Englishman come out from within this mild ox-driver, and they did not want to see it again, especially directed at themselves.

Hob was vaguely aware of them, but he did not care: Nemain had explained to him once how she and her grandmother spoke to animals, how the words were not important, only the tone and the force of the will. Of course they were both adepts of the Art, but the principle, she had assured him, worked on a more mundane level as well, and he of all people had the ox's trust.

Finally the ox put a hoof to the board; hearing it boom and seeing the ramp quiver stopped him for a moment, but then he essayed another footstep, and yet another, and then he just walked the rest of the way, turning his head about as he emerged on deck, snuffing deeply of the fresh salt air of the harbor.

Hob led him across the deck to the down ramp, and there was another discussion about stepping off the ship. When at last the timid giant had reached the dock, he took a few steps, and then staggered. He walked forward a few paces, but then had to dance in place to maintain his balance. After the constant motion of the deck had come to seem almost normal, to have the fixed earth beneath him was disorienting to the ox, as it is to many travelers. Milo took the sensible course and lay down in his tracks till the earth should cease its strange behavior. Hob tethered him to a dockside bollard and went to help Jack, who was bringing off the little ass Mavourneen and the mare Tapaigh.

The captain, Master Hugh, stood by the rail saying his farewells to Molly and Nemain, with promises of free passage should they return to England.

"'Tis a grand offer," said Molly, "but I'm hoping we'll make our home here for aye." An innocent comment, the hope of an exile coming home to stay, as Nemain pointed out that night, with no mention of the necessity of destroying an outlawed clan of violent usurpers.

Molly had Sweetlove under one arm, the little dog craning her neck to follow Jack's movements. She would endure being held by Molly, but was never happy away from Jack. Redmane was trailing along after Hob, and after they got the docile Mavourneen off the boat with no trouble, he let his daughter hold the little ass's lead rope down on the dock, while he went back and, with Jack, encouraged the more skittish mare to step onto the creaking, flexing planks of the ramp.

The other draft animals were not as affected as Milo, and by the time Hob and Jack had them hitched to the small and midsized wagons, the ox was on his feet again, and Hob hitched him to the main wagon. Eventually they were ready to move: Molly was up on the driver's seat of the big wagon, followed by the small wagon, with Nemain and Redmane driving Mavourneen, and finally the midsized wagon, Jack and Sweetlove up on the box behind Tapaigh.

Hob took up the lead rope: Milo could be driven from the big wagon's seat, but took direction better from being led, especially by Hob. This also added to Hob's ability to pass unnoticed as the husband and father in a small traveling troupe of entertainers and healers. Had he assumed his identity of Sir Robert, a Norman knight, the disparity in social station between himself and his ostensible inferiors would have been noticed.

Adam and his nephew were on the dock, watching and fretting over each barrel of wine rolled down the ramp, each bale of silks wrapped in leather being lowered from a wooden boom to dockside, the rope squeaking through the pulley, men with upstretched arms ready to guide it to a growing stack. Murchad had a square of pale wood on which, with a thin stick of charcoal, he marked off items as they were unloaded. Now his uncle noticed that Molly's troupe was preparing to move off the dock. He nudged Murchad, causing a smudged entry and a *tsk* of exasperation from the younger man, and then both were hurrying to say farewells.

Adam looked up to Molly on the driver's seat of the main wagon. "If it please you, Mistress, may we recommend the inn we are to stay at, Mistress Lavin's Inn? 'Tis run by Irish, and 'tis friendly to Irish custom."

Here he glanced about to see that he was not overheard. All around was a bustle of activity: dockworkers stacking cargo, seamen lowering goods from the hold, Norman customs officials walking about with their lists; there were shouts, the bang of heavy objects on the wooden pier, the rasp of the ropes through the sheaves, the rumble of wheels from the haulers' wains arriving and departing. No one was paying attention, and no one could have heard Adam by accident.

"Dublin is your Norman town, isn't it, and the Normans not fond of us Irish. Oh, 'tis fine if you're an Englishman, or one of the old Ostmen, those Danes that settled here in Viking times, or a Welshman, or a Fleming, but there's been too much blood spilled between the Irish and the Dublin Normans, and 'tis best if you keep to yourself, and behave quietly, and do not come within the ken of the city watch."

It had been a long time since Molly had been through Dublin, and now she said, "'Tis good to know all this, and to know where we're to settle for the night, instead of wandering the streets with all these wagons seeking an inn, and I thank you, Master Adam."

"And, and . . ." said Adam, and faltered.

"And what, friend Adam?" said Molly in her most encouraging voice.

"The four of you, and Master Robert, Robert the Englishman . . . well, these are unsettled times in Erin, and we must fare far to the west, and might we but travel together, my nephew and I would feel ourselves better protected, surely. We're part of the Tribes of Galway, do you see, and it's guards they'll be hiring as well, but not all of them stay hired, do you see, and to know that you're two men we can trust, and two women skilled at the bow as well, then, then, do you see . . ."

He looked up at her with the rest of his plea in his eyes if not on his lips.

Molly said, "Friend Adam, it's delighted we'll be to travel with you, for the company and for our own protection." And as she told her family later, it would provide a cloak that would help to keep them unremarked: their wagons in among other wagons, their group blended in with the folk of the merchants' caravan.

"That's grand, then," said Adam. "Isn't it grand, Murchad?"

"Oh, aye," said his nephew, looking up from his tally board. A more practical sort, he began to describe how to reach Mistress Lavin's Inn.

"Go up here—you can take Winetavern Street or Fishamble, and when you come to John's Lane . . ."

Dublin was a city comparable to York in size. Fish shops were clustered along the waterfront area, tanners' goods and woven wool were sold in shops a bit farther from the Liffey. There were goldsmiths and the more usual blacksmiths, bakers, leatherworkers, rope walks and harness makers, cow keepers with milk cows in the backyards who sold milk at the front door, grain sellers, wine sellers and food shops, butchers, taverns. The throngs along the narrow streets spoke English and Irish and a patois of both; Hob could also hear the guttural accents of the Ostmen, the "East-men" as the descendants of the Vikings called themselves—they thought of the Irish as "West-men"—and the lilt of Welsh. Mailed Norman knights rode down the center of the streets, the iron shoes on the horses thudding in the dirt of the way;

Christian priests telling their beads walked past shaggy-headed Irish workers loading grain sacks onto the beds of tall-wheeled wains. Alewives with their barrows called out their wares in musical voices, making what were near-songs of their offerings.

Hob found progress even slower than it had been through the streets of York when they'd passed through that city some years back. At a crossroads they had to wait while drovers moved a flock of sheep across their path; at a place where the street they followed curved around a churchyard, two wains had tangled their wheels. One wheel had broken and the heavy wooden spokes penetrated the spaces between the spokes on the other wain; there was much cursing in Irish and in Norman English, and eventually the one wain had to be unloaded to make it light enough for men to wrench it free of the other.

A small crowd gathered, calling advice to the wagoners, mixed with humorous unhelpful comments; Hob amused himself, as their little three-wagon caravan stood becalmed, with observing the Dublin citizenry as they enjoyed this bit of impromptu entertainment. At last a call for volunteers went up, and enough broad-backed men stepped forward and took hold of the unloaded wain. A voice was lifted in a chant, the crowd heaved, relaxed, heaved again, and the wain was rocked loose. The undamaged wain was then free to proceed, clearing half the street, and Hob clucked to Milo, who had begun to doze in place, and they set off again.

Two more turns and down a smaller lane, and here was Mistress Lavin's Inn. Hob went in and made arrangements with the innkeeper, a large jolly woman with a merry laugh; following her directions, he went out and led Milo, and thus the caravan, around the corner to the broad entrance to the innyard. Soon they had the wagons chocked in one corner of the yard, had the beasts stabled, and had a table to themselves.

Here came the innkeeper's cousin, a young woman of perhaps twenty summers, bearing dishes of venison sausage and bowls of stirabout—oatmeal porridge, in this case with an *annlann*, or flavoring, of golden butter. She set out trenchers at each place, scurried off and was back in almost no time with jacks of barley beer for the adults and buttermilk for Redmane. Sweetlove jumped up on the bench beside Jack and sat looking alertly at the table. Jack gave her a sausage, and she settled down with it between her front paws, daintily biting off a piece at a time.

Soon they had finished, and Macha Redmane, tired from the traveling and the excitement, had climbed into her great-grandmother's ample lap. Molly held her with one hand and with the other stroked her hair rhythmically, hypnotically; soon she was dozing against Molly's bosom. The others were just sitting back, sipping at the last of the beer, when Adam and his nephew came in, the latter immediately half tripping on a bench leg and barely recovering.

Molly's troupe had not seen them since the dock, where they were overseeing the loading of their cargo into wains. The two men had then seen the wains conveyed to a safe warehouse. Later guards and drivers hired by the *Treibheanna na Gaillimhe*, the Tribes of Galway, would be assembled, and the two would set out in a caravan to that city in the West of Ireland. Adam and Murchad were members of one of the Tribes, and they were bringing the present cargo home to the Galway warehouses.

From the Dublin warehouse they had plainly stopped to investigate some few taverns on the way here. Adam's eyes had the slightly glassy, not-quite-seeing appearance that a great many mugs of strong drink will produce, and his nephew, whose hair was in damp disarray, some locks adhering to his forehead and others jutting out at odd angles here and there, lurched when he walked and swayed when he stood still. When he saw Molly's people, Murchad's eyes lit up, and he hailed them loudly from some distance away. They made their way with a great deal of difficulty down the long room, sat down heavily on the empty end of Hob's bench, and called for *uisce beatha*.

When Aednat, the young cousin, appeared with mugs of the fiery liquid, Adam stood and toasted Molly's family: "Our saviors," and then Murchad stood, somewhat precariously, and singled out Hob in a long and rambling tribute, calling him "Robert the Englishman" and "the Sea-Butcher," and much else. The other patrons in the common room began to take notice, turning on their benches, and Molly and her family became increasingly concerned at the amount of attention the pair were provoking.

At last Molly managed to quiet them down, and to lean in conspiratorily. She dropped her voice, which had the effect of making the two merchants draw close and keep quiet, in order to hear her.

" 'Tis that we have enemies, and we're not wanting them to know of us, and of where we are," she said. "If you've gratitude for your lives, show it by holding your tongue for a year and a day. After that, you may speak of it as you will. But for now, especially do not describe me."

Both managed to look owlishly serious.

"Aye, Mistress."

"We swear, Mistress. But . . ."

"But?" Molly asked, her eyebrows rising.

"We have mayhap said somewhat of our adventure, um, here and there, tonight . . ."

"What's done is done, but from now on, be my friends and say naught."

Now that they were on land again, and settled at the inn, Hob and Nemain were able to be alone with each other, sleeping in the midsized wagon while Molly took Macha Redmane into the big wagon, and Jack settled himself to sleep in the little wagon, Sweetlove arranging herself in a coil on his back, or curved on the pillow around the top of his head, or slumped against his side, as the mood took her.

For Hob it was a joy once again to taste the delights of the marriage bed: Nemain's small smooth body, the softness of her skin beneath which was the muscle of a young battle queen, the long red cape of her hair, the enthusiasm with which she explored his own body, and the near frenzy that she worked herself up to at the finish.

She had drifted away into sleep, and he lay looking at

shifting patterns of shadow on the wall of the wagon opposite the window. The shutters were open a bit on a chain, and moonlight filtered in through the trees growing just over the innyard wall, and a small breeze moved the branches, and the shadows always seemed just about to tell him something.

There was a subtle difference to the scent of the late spring in Ireland—some difference in what grew here, perhaps—and he thought, We are here at last, after so much venturing toward this goal! He heard a faint rhythmic sound: Nemain was snoring, a delicate high sound, soothing, familiar.

He said a silent Paternoster and an *Ave*, asked the Sieur Jesus for help in their quest, including the deaths of their enemies, asked Him to overlook his wife and her grandmother's pagan beliefs, asked Him to make him a better father and husband, and, unable to think of anything else to pester the Lord with, rolled on his side, and slid into sleep.

Chapter 5

When they had spent a day resting and acquiring some provisions for the journey to the West, Molly announced that she wanted to take a walk about Dublin, to see what had changed since the last time she had been there, and that she'd like the others, even Redmane, to come with her, "for 'tis good that the child should see this city, and 'tis uncertain when we'll return here."

They locked the wagons with Jack's war hammer and Hob's longsword inside, for the streets were fairly safe by day: the Normans kept a standing watch that patrolled with pole arms, and serious disorder was not tolerated. Sweetlove was in the big wagon with her water bowl and a bone to keep her occupied; Hob and Jack had made sure the draft animals were comfortable in the stables—fed, watered, brushed. The little family strolled north from Mistress Lavin's Inn, and then wandered west, past Christ Church Cathedral. North on Bridge Street and so over Dublin Bridge, now known as King John's Bridge, since their old enemy had rebuilt it in wood and stone.

From the north side of the bridge they wandered into Ostmantown; as the Normans took control of Dublin, the descendants of the Viking founders, now mixed with the Gaelic Irish, had moved to the fields north of the river. Here there was the sound of Gaelic spoken in harsh accents, with the occasional Danish word still used. Molly seemed to have some destination in mind, and the party strolled farther and farther north.

Macha Redmane, as always, was interested in everything and wanted an explanation of how it worked. They paused at a cooper's yard to watch the staves being set into hoops, Redmane reluctant to leave until she'd seen at least one barrel completed, and then it was necessary to examine the wares set out at a goldsmith's window, the jewelry worked into the sinuous patterns favored by the Celts.

In general Molly, without urging undue haste, had kept them moving on, but here, where the merchant had opened his horizontal shutters, the bottom leaf propped to form a display shelf and the top leaf chained up to make a sheltering awning, was something that both women were as interested in as the child. At once three heads were bent over the bracelets, armlets, earrings, and necklaces spaced evenly on a cloth of black wool. There was much picking up and examining of the wares, trying on of armlet and necklace, comparing items, while Jack and Hob kept an eye on the street, partly from old habits of caution, partly from boredom.

At one point Hob looked over at Jack; the man-at-arms just gave a shrug: What can one do? Eventually the women bought a filigree bracelet for Redmane, the goldsmith tightening it to fit her slender wrist.

They moved on past a few more shops—more goldsmiths, some silversmiths, and a smattering of whitesmiths—and turned into a street loud with the bang and clank of hammers on iron and steel. The constant ringing of metal against metal made a kind of music; a thin haze of smoke hung in the air all down the way. This was Blacksmith Lane, lined with forges, their big doors open to the street. Some of the smiths had their anvils set up in the open doorways, partly to get away from the heat of the bellows-whipped forges.

By the nature of their work, blacksmiths tended to be large, burly men, and as they made their way down the street, Hob's and Jack's interest picking up at the displays of weapons and tools set out on wooden benches, they came upon the father of all smiths, an enormous black-bearded man with heavily muscled arms and a large belly restrained by a broad leather belt. His anvil was set up in the shop entrance, almost in the street, and he was pounding on the blade of a billhook, the farmer's curved pruning knife. The metal was still glowing from the forge; he clutched the rat-tail tang in a pair of heavy wooden-handled pliers.

Molly drifted up to his display bench, and picked up an axhead, a wedge-shaped piece of metal in the Danish style with a ring socket for fastening it to a haft. She tested the edge with her thumb, and struck the blade with one of her rings, and then tossed it down contemptuously. The smith kept working, although he struck somewhat more slowly, and he watched her from the side of his eyes.

"Is this the best of your work, then?" she asked coldly.

Hob, who was now competent if a little halting in his ability to speak Irish, was surprised, indeed shocked, at Molly's tone: normally she was open and friendly to strangers unless they proved hostile in some way. The smith threw down his hammer. He waited till a knot of three men, looking at the wares spread out in front of the shops, had moved on past, and then:

"Come; I'll show you my best," he said, and gestured into the depths of his shop, where apprentices and journeymen labored at the forge. He did not have the guttural Norse-Gael accent; his Irish sounded to Hob like that of his wife and her grandmother.

He glanced over at Nemain; she was looking hard at the smith, and suddenly Hob's suspicions were aroused. He rested his hand on the leather-wrapped hilt of his war dagger. Molly was a formidable woman, but the smith was a mountain of a man, and he had accomplices inside. Hob said to Redmane, "Stay here a moment, culver, we'll be back anon."

But the smith threw up a hand, palm out, toward him. "Just her," he said curtly.

Before Hob or Nemain could protest, Molly said quietly, "They are my people."

And with that, the smith grunted, turned his broad back, and walked away into the dimness of the smithy.

"Bring the child," said Molly. "I'll not have her wait alone in the street."

Hob followed her into the heat of the shop. Two apprentices worked a wheezing leather bellows; the forge glowed white-hot; two journeymen with tongs were heating the ends of iron bars. There were two more anvils within the shop, and on one of them another journeyman was pounding a yellow-hot bar into a rough flat strip, sparks showering down to the packed-earth floor. Mixed with the inevitable scent of smoke was the subtle tang of very hot metal. The walls of the shop were hung with leather that had been wetted. In the rear wall was an arch with a separate door cloth of damp leather, and this the smith raised and held aside for Molly.

She passed through, and the huge man continued to hold it, gesturing impatiently for the others to go through, all the while scowling at them. They entered, Nemain with her arm around Macha's shoulders, Hob next, Jack coming last, keeping the smith in sight at all times. The smith followed them in, dropping the leather behind them. They all stood uncertainly in a dark corridor, and the blacksmith pushed his way to the front and led them farther into what must be a rather long building.

Another archway, another hanging—this one a woven cloth—and they were in a back room with three crude chairs, a very long table, some benches.

Hob looked around: Where were the other wares promised, "my best"? Every muscle in his body tensed, and he prepared to spring upon the smith, his hand already beginning to slide the war dagger from its sheath. Then he stopped, utterly astonished.

For the smith had thrown himself to his knees in front of Molly, and he grasped her right hand in both of his paws, and kissed it, and burst into a storm of weeping.

"Bróccan, Bróccan," Molly murmured, stroking his head with her free hand, gazing down at him with every indication of fondness.

Bróccan coughed and snuffled and released her hand to wipe at his eyes. "We thought you were gone for aye," he managed to say, and then had to wait again to gain control of himself.

"Up, lad; come now, my dear," said Molly, and he lumbered to his feet and stood gazing at her mutely. "We have returned but a few days ago, but things will be different now, here and in the West."

She turned to the others. "Bróccan here is one of the council members of our clan, and an important man in it, and escaped the slaughter of our underchiefs by mere chance, as did Nemain and myself. I had had word he was dwelling here in Ostmantown, and hiding among the Normans for safety from our enemies—they are men who forestall revenge by killing every last one of their victims."

Bróccan was plainly disoriented by the shock, and by the effort it took to conceal his first reaction out in the street, for now he looked at Redmane and said to Molly, "Is this little Nemain?"

Almost at once he caught himself. "Nay, it cannot be."

Now he looked at Nemain, and he said, "By She Whom I swear by, it must be this young woman."

Molly laughed. "You have it now, my heart. The years go by and the crops grow in the fields. This is her daughter, Macha Redmane."

"Do you remembering him, sweeting?" Hob asked Nemain in his awkward Irish.

"Aye, it's now that I recall him; when first I saw him outside I had a strange feeling that I knew him and knew him not. I was so young when we left. . . ."

Bróccan came to Nemain and went to one knee; he kissed her hand and said, "My queen." Then he did the same for little Macha. Her tiny hand lay upon his broad palm, scarred with cuts and burns from the forge, and he bent his shaggy head over it, thus swearing fealty to three generations of chieftain.

Bróccan stood; he drew a great breath and looked around. "Sit you down, kinfolk, sit, and I'll bring drink." He went into the next room and came back with a jug: from the beads of moisture on it, it must have been sitting in cold water. He set out mugs for the company, stepped to the curtain, and bellowed, "Aidan!" Then he gave a mug to Molly and filled it from the jug. He served Nemain, Jack, and Hob in that order, and hesitated when he came to Macha Redmane.

"A little water for the child would be well," said Nemain.

"Och, aye," said the smith, and just then a lad of perhaps fourteen put his head in at the door cloth.

"Run upstairs and fetch your mother," said Bróccan. "We have guests."

"Yes, Father," said Aidan, and disappeared. When Redmane had been given her water, the smith stood and lifted his mug to Molly. "To my queen and chief, and to our clan!" he said, and drank. They all followed suit, and Hob discovered that his mug contained undiluted *uisce beatha*, the welcome warmth sliding down his throat, the sweet delicate aftertaste lingering pleasantly.

And here came Aidan with a woman in her midthirties, flushed from haste, who threw herself on Molly and hugged her, then in some confusion tried to kneel, but was raised up by Molly and hugged again.

"Fiadh, my heartbeat, 'tis good to look upon you once more," said Molly.

"Och, have you come to lead us home, Grandmother?" asked the woman, smiling the while, but with tears running down her cheeks and a catch in her voice. She used the Ó Cearbhaills' familiar title of respect for their elder queen: since the tribe were all related to one another, their matriarch was thought of, was respected as, was loved as a literal grandmother would be. The younger Nemain would be addressed as "Mother," or the affectionate "Little Mother," no matter the age of the speaker relative to the queen.

"I have that," said Molly, "but we must move slowly and silently at first, as a wildcat creeping toward her prey, so that when we spring 'twill be a surprise to our foes—they are not easy to kill, and we do not want them forewarned, with their sorcery and their gallowglasses."

Bróccan paused with his mug of the lifewater at his lips.

"Those queens—you know that two of them are in Dublin Castle this day, do you not?"

"Nay—here, you say?"

"Their war queen, Ferelith, is here with the half-wild younger sister, Malmhìn. The Normans up to the castle, they're after hearing of my skills, and sending for me, and the upshot is that I do smithing for them, and I teach some of their apprentices in the stables, shoeing horses and making the ironware for the harnesses, and the like. And so I'm hearing and seeing some of what passes, and the stables against the bailey wall as they are, I'm seeing who comes and goes." He nodded at his wife. "And Fiadh's cousin's daughter is a serving maid at the castle as well, and she hearing all that transpires at the castle, with her own ears or afterward, listening to the kitchen gossip."

Fiadh gave a little start at the word *kitchen*. "But let me not have you sitting to an empty table!" she exclaimed. "Aidan, fetch your sister!" And with that, she rushed out into the next room; by the sound of it, she continued into another room beyond that.

Bróccan looked after her for a moment, then leaned forward, dropping his voice a bit. "They two queens are here to gain Norman support, for already the neighboring clans grow weary of them. There has been some cattle raiding, and some strange killings, and they are so fell a clan, with their mailed gallowglasses and the eldest sister a powerful sorceress, that there is talk of a joint campaign against them. So they seek some aid from the Lord of Dublin, and mayhap from King Henry away in London. This is all the doing of

Ferelith, for the youngest sister is too strange to treat with the Normans of Dublin, much less London. In truth I believe that Ferelith did not dare to leave her unwatched at home, and so brought her here."

"Cannot the eldest sister keep her in check, then?" asked Molly.

"From what I am to hear, the eldest keeps herself apart, in a cave filled with cats, near the oceanside cliffs, and works her sorceries, some of them terrible indeed," said the smith, lowering his voice yet again, and even looking about, as if fearing to see the eldest sister appear in a corner.

"Filled with cats?" said Nemain.

"She is said to be under a *geis*, that never may she harm a cat; 'tis one condition of her strength in the Art. 'Tis a bargain made with some Power—if I understand it aright," said Bróccan, somewhat diffident about discussing what were essentially women's mysteries before Molly, whom he knew to be an adept, and Nemain—as Molly's granddaughter she might be assumed to be a worker of the Art as well.

"A *geis*—that is something that must to doing, is it not?" asked Hob in his imperfect Irish.

"'Tis something that must be done, or must be avoided doing," said Molly to Hob. "I have heard of her *geis*, from the Beekeeper. She's after doing some bargain with a Power or Powers, to be so very strong, and 'tis not that I know which One she's protected by. Her *geis* is to protect all cats that come to her, and let no harm nor hunger come to them, and she's indeed ever surrounded by them, and I've heard that some of the cats are not true cats, but . . . Something Else."

She turned to Bróccan. "This is Sir Robert, my granddaughter's husband, and like a son to me," said Molly. "For now we are keeping ourselves quiet as field mice, as we did in England, and you may address me as Molly"—for Bróccan knew her as Maeve, his queen, his clan chief—"and we will not give out that he is a belted knight, but only a common Englishman, Robert."

"You came in a few days past?" asked Bróccan slowly.

"We did that," said Molly.

"Was it that you were troubled with pirates?" asked the smith.

"We were."

"A common Englishman—is this then 'Robert the Englishman' who is spoken of in all the taverns?"

Molly looked unhappy. "Ochone! And we hoping to escape notice! Those loose-lips, those merchants, have spread their tales throughout Dublin on their drunken strolls."

"Throughout Dublin, and even unto the castle itself. There are tales of a prodigious slaughter by Robert the Englishman, and of women archers cutting men down right and left, and of an ogre with a hammer whom none could get nigh."

"This is my man, Jack Brown, and as you can see he's a fine-looking fellow, and no ogre atall, but even you, Bróccan, would not care to come nigh his war hammer."

Bróccan bowed to the two men. "You will want to keep these two men from the young queen's grasp, and especially Sir Ro—sure I mean to say Robert the Englishman. She is said to be afire to meet this killer—'tis the thought of all that blood on his hands that provokes her."

"If that excites her, she must be a strange creature indeed," said Nemain icily.

"She is like a woodland creature, Little Mother," said the smith to her. "I have heard that back in the West, in our homeland, they can barely keep her dressed, and she runs wild through the forest, and is gone for days at a time, none knows where."

He peered into the doorway, but his wife was not in evidence. "She is . . . 'tis difficult to say, but . . . she is well nigh overwhelming to men. She is a handsome woman, although very wild in appearance, and she has an . . . odor . . . 'tis a musky womanly odor, and I found my own loins stirred, and she but prowling past the stables, with her walk like a lynx and her dark hungry eyes. I'm not an old man, mind, but I'm no longer in hot youth, and married, and with bairns of my own. Yet . . ."

He paused a moment, with the vague look of someone gazing at a memory instead of what lies before him. Then he came to himself, and cast a look of concern at Macha Redmane.

"She's wise beyond her years," said Nemain, "and she's not one to repeat what's been heard."

"Aye, well . . ." The blacksmith seemed embarrassed by his confession. "'Tis that I wanted to warn you, and especially your men here, that 'tis a strange power she has, and it comes upon you all swiftly, and 'tis well to be braced against it."

" 'Tis always well to know somewhat of the enemy," said Molly. "Have you had word of any of our kin, scattered as they are?"

"There are several here in Dublin that I see—they come to the forge, or we meet in the taverns—and others that they know, scattered through Erin. Some have taken service on ships, and we see them when they are in port. There is a band of the younger men, led by Fergal—you remember Fergal? He was but a youth when we dispersed—who hire out to the Tribes of Galway as horse guards for their caravans. Most have settled here and there along the eastern coast, working on others' farms, for fear of being hunted down by the Uí Bháis."

Molly drew a heavy silver ring, ornately worked, from her right hand. "Here, Bróccan my child, take this as a sign from me, show it to every one of our kin that you meet, and have each one seek out any that he knows, and bid the clan make ready, for soon we will muster in the West, and some Norman friends of mine will aid us with a muster of knights and men-at-arms and archers, and we have allies even amid the Church itself."

The smith closed it in his great fist. "I will tell those I know, and bid them send the word throughout Erin. Soon we will be ready."

Fiadh reappeared, with a girl about sixteen following her, the two with plates of cold cooked meats kept chilled in crocks submerged in the stream that gurgled behind the smithy—rabbit, venison, pork. They had also steaming bowls of the omnipresent oatmeal porridge with butter and cheese.

They spread cloths on the long table, set out places, then left and reappeared with pitchers of barley beer, and for Redmane, a cup of buttermilk. Smiths in general tended to prosper, and Bróccan was among the best, and could afford his own two milk cows in a byre out back.

In a short time, all was ready, benches and chairs were drawn up, and Molly's family seated. Fiadh and her helper, who proved to be Aidan's sister, Morna, served them while Bróccan carved meat at the end of the table. Molly was seated at the head of the table, with Nemain at her right hand.

Bróccan called Aidan in, and bade him have the journeymen close down the forge for the day, and send the apprentices home, and come back to the table. Today was a great day, and called for a feast and a celebration, and talk of better days to come, and plans for revenge.

Chapter 6

When the caravan of merchants, including Adam and his nephew Murchad, had been formed up in the street outside the warehouses maintained by the Tribes of Galway, the fourteen great merchant families of that city, Molly's three wagons were stationed near the rear of the line. Adam had been delighted at the presence of one whom he termed "the great butcher of the Irish Sea," as he described Robert the Englishman. Hob was increasingly known by this name in the taverns of Dublin, thanks to the tireless tongue of Murchad and the inevitable exaggeration of the already formidable victory over the Manx pirates.

Of course the caravan had its usual guards as well—household kerns of the Tribes, augmented by Irish mercenaries. Mounted on their agile if somewhat small Irish horses, these escorts exuded a dashing self-confidence, riding bare-legged, clad in the *léine*, the long Irish tunic, with a voluminous cloak cast about their shoulders and secured with a ring brooch. They rode without stirrups, seated on woolen pads instead of saddles; for arms they bore three light javelins, held in a deep quiver secured across each back; a sword and a heavy dagger adorned each belt. Drooping moustaches fell past their chins, and their hair hung shaggy and uncombed, cut short at their foreheads for visibility. In addition to their uncut locks, some had long thin braids that hung down from their temples, weighted by a pierced coin or the skull of a raven or a weasel.

They rolled out on a fine morning through St. Nicholas's Gate. They were following a trade route worked out by the Tribes some time past, with scheduled stops at inns and hostels partly maintained by cooperative mercantile groups. Up past the top end of the coastal mountains that lay west and south of Dublin, into the central plain of Ireland, with its bogs and extensive forests, haunted by bandits, hostile Irish tribesmen, Norman robber barons. The Irish escorts, swift and agile, were more suited to the boggy terrain and thick woodland than were the heavily armed Norman knights on their huge destriers—less apt to become mired in muddy ground, swifter to respond to attacks up or down the long caravan.

Molly's destination lay on the coast, not too far from Galway; they were to stay at St. Mary's, a priory of the Benedictines. The rendezvous with Sir Jehan and the other Normans, coming as they were by coaster round the south of Ireland, was set at the nearby castle of the FitzAnthonys, friends of Sir Odinell. They would bring with them Hob's destrier, Iarann, and his armor. Hob would then transform himself from the role of traveler in Molly's troupe of healers and musicians to his actual station of Norman knight, as Molly and Nemain would resume their rightful places as queens and tribal chieftains.

Hob walked along as usual, leading stolid Milo with a rope—a more effective way of guiding the powerful but somewhat dreamy animal than using the reins. Molly thus had little to do but work the brake, and watch for any danger along the road. The ox drew Molly's big wagon, and Nemain and Redmane followed, up on the seat of the small wagon, drawn by Mavourneen, an ass who was as much Nemain's pet as a worker. Last came the midsized wagon, drawn by the mare Tapaigh, driven by Jack, with the terrier Sweetlove curled on the seat beside him.

The first day passed without incident. They started early, and the morning was fine: the sun sparkling off the Liffey, small birds singing in the hedges, the sweet scent of green Erin. A little after midday there was a rain so fine and gentle that Hob thought it more like a drifting heavy mist than rain. Halfway through the afternoon the sun reappeared, the leaves of the trees and bushes alongside the trail glinting like jewels as the sunlight tangled in the beads of moisture that had collected there. Then toward sunset a thin rain began again. That was Erin, Molly told him later that night: rain, and sun, and then rain again.

At evening there was shouting up ahead, and then the wagons began turning in to a wide compound surrounded by wooden walls. The ground around had been cleared of brush and other cover, and the walls—constructed of logs twice the height of a tall man, sunk into the earth—had a walkway that ran all around the inside perimeter, so that bowmen could command the approaches to the compound. There was an associated inn for the drivers, the merchants, and the escort. Guards employed at the compound manned the walls, so that the escort might rest for the night.

They were assigned a place for the wagons, and Hob and Jack unhitched the animals and led them to the inn's stables. The Tribes' drivers and their helpers were here, crowding into the central aisle that led to the stalls. Mostly the wains were drawn by oxen, like Milo, but in two-ox teams; some few were pulled by horses. There was much banter and horseplay, and Hob had to make his way patiently down the aisle till he could find a free stall for Milo. At one point he had to just wait till a knot of two drivers and two helpers with four oxen untangled itself and the animals were slotted into their respective stalls. As Molly had instructed him, Hob kept an ear on the drivers' conversations, to see if anything might be learned about the doings of the Uí Bháis, but there was nothing but casual greeting, professional chatter about the draft animals and the gear, and some unusually bawdy humor from the younger men.

At last they were free to go to dinner. Molly and Nemain had been preparing the beds in the wagons. Jack had constructed them so that, with a minimum of clearing away of things used during the day, the beds could be swung down from their fastenings on the wall. The bed in each wagon was set with one long side against the wall, with sturdy hinges, so that by heaving them up and swiveling wooden lock bars at each end, they would be out of the way when not in use. Now the women went from wagon to wagon, each taking one end of the bed, turning the wooden lock bars so that the bed came free, lowering the bed, and spreading blankets, while Redmane bustled about placing pillows and draping the head cloths used to cover those pillows.

When the men returned from the stables, the whole family set off for the inn's common room. Dinner was simple but hearty: oat cakes with salt butter, black pudding made with pork, carrots and peas, dried apples. Molly's troupe repaired to the wagons, and slept with locked doors and the shutters on short chains, but they were safe enough in the Tribes' compound, under the Tribes' paternal eye.

THE NEXT FEW DAYS found the column skirting a vast bog, using guides hired by the Tribes. Soon thereafter came the feared attack, masterless Irish kerns leaping from ambush behind the dense hedges that grew to one side of the road. In a moment they had flung their light javelins, knocking two drivers from their seats. Men sprang to the draft horses' heads and attempted to lead them into the forest on the far side of the path.

A moment later Hob had his sword out and Molly had turned and retrieved her bow and quiver from the hatch at the front of the big wagon. She climbed swiftly up the rope ladder to the wagon roof. Nemain had lifted Redmane into the small wagon through the hatch and the child handed her out her bow and quiver.

Behind them all, Jack had gotten Sweetlove inside the wagon, come out with his crow-beak war hammer, and limped up along the line, fastening each of Molly's wagons to the one ahead, which prevented easy theft.

The escort came sweeping down the line, hacking down from their saddles at the thieves, who were all afoot. Hob saw one of the mounted guards, up at the next wagon ahead, pulled from his saddle by a kern with a billhook, a farmer's weapon, a sickle on the end of a spear shaft. The guard rolled, half-stunned, on the ground, and the bandit raised his weapon for a killing stroke. Hob reached him before he could bring the bill down, and without compunction ran the man through from behind. The guard took Hob's hand, struggled to his feet, and pressed a bunched fold of his mantle against the cut the hook had made in his shoulder, not serious but bleeding freely.

A second group of the marauders had run around the hedge and appeared in the rear of the column, intending to surprise the defenders with an attack from a new direction. There was only one wagon behind Jack's tailboard; otherwise Molly's three wagons were the last in the column. The driver of the wagon behind was quickly put down, and two bandits set about pulling the horses into the woods, while the rest of the bandit force, some six or seven, pressed on to Jack's wagon.

This of course was a great miscalculation on their part. Even as Hob was heading back to help the dark man, Nemain had put a black-feathered arrow into the lead bandit, and then Jack was among them: the hammerhead dashed the brains from the next brigand, and the crow-beak swept back on the return stroke to tear at the throat of the kern beside him. Seven bandits had now become four in as many heartbeats, and here came Hob, roaring, "*Banríon Maeve abú!*" with his longsword raised on high, even as Nemain pierced another man at the rear, the arrow hissing over Hob's head and thudding into the kern's chest. A kern stabbed overhand at Jack with a light spear, and Jack smashed the spearpoint into the ground with his hammer, stepped in and smote the man on the jaw with a fist like a riverbed rock. He fell, and Hob put the sword into him.

The remaining two kerns, side by side, were already backing away when a group of three horse guards swept past Hob and Jack and stabbed the kerns to death with javelins. The horsemen swerved into the woods, pursuing those who had made off with wagons.

A strange calm settled over the caravan, after so much shouting and the clang of weapons. Somewhere up forward someone was crying out in pain, but gradually that was muted. The wagonmaster, a graying experienced retainer of the Tribes, came riding back with a small work party. The bodies of those caravan members who were slain—four drivers, a guard, a merchant's factor—were wrapped in coarse cloth and put in one of the wains for burial; the bodies of bandits were hauled a short way under the trees and left.

In a little while the guards who had headed off in pursuit returned, having regained two of the three stolen wagons;

presumably the thieves who had taken them were killed or had fled. The third wagon had vanished into the bandit-haunted forest, along paths that only they would know.

The wagonmaster headed back up the column, and shortly the wagons in line ahead began to move, and Hob tugged Milo into motion westward; they were on their way again, across Ireland to the great Western Ocean.

Chapter 7

Molly had pointed out one evening, back in Dublin, that she was the only one who could be recognized by their old enemies. Nemain had been but a child when they left, and Jack and Hob had never set foot in Erin before, so if they should encounter one of the Uí Bháis, especially one of the three queens, it was agreed that Molly would retire to the big wagon, and if any of the merchants should ask, it would be given out that she was unwell. While the story of Robert the Englishman and his deeds of slaughter aboard *la Gracedieux* had already escaped into popular gossip, she had warned Adam and Murchad that under no circumstances should they describe her. She had put it so strongly that it would not be untrue to say that she had frightened the two men; in addition, she had described the two queens known to be in Dublin and charged them to warn her should they come near the inn.

But discovery by the foe was not at all expected to be a problem once they were safely on the road—not, at least, till they gained the coast, and were ready to begin overt hostilities. So it was a great surprise, two nights after the bandit attack, secure for the night in Diarmuid's Inn, one of the contracted way stations of the Tribes of Galway, at dinner in the common room, when Murchad came in and hastily made his way to Molly's side. He sat sideways on the bench and said, "Mistress, there's a mort of gallowglasses have just sounded the horn and been admitted; they're stabling their mounts now and there's a travelling wagon, and the curtain drawn back a moment, and wasn't there a strange woman gazing forth, wild-haired, with a fierce and cunning look to her eyes, and I'm thinking this is one of those you warned against."

Molly was sitting with her little family, spreading a bit of the rich golden Irish butter on a piece of dark onion-studded bread for Redmane, and she quickly handed the morsel to the girl, kissed her head, and got up from the bench, almost all in one motion. "It's in the wagon I'll be," she said to Nemain. "You know what to do and say if it comes to speaking with them. Friend Murchad, you have done well." She embraced him quickly and left for the innyard and the large wagon. Hob knew that if she wished not to be seen, she could slip from shadow to shadow like a hunter, and he forced himself to continue calmly with his meal.

"So you've seeing her?" asked Hob, and then corrected

himself. "Seen her. What is she like, then, this woman?" Murchad stopped a serving-lad and told him to bring ale. He looked around. "I've a young wife," he said, as though defending himself against a charge that no one had made. He drew a circle on the table with his forefinger, then another. "She's a comely woman," he said, looking at the tabletop. "Strange woman, strange, but . . ."

"Is the other queen with her?" asked Nemain.

Murchad was still distracted, thinking of the woman he had seen. No doubt, thought Hob, he feels the pull that Bróccan spoke of. Murchad roused himself.

"Nay, she has come away early by herself," he said. "I lingered awhile, nearby, because— Well, I was nearby and I heard her speaking to the wagonmaster, and she saying she wished to travel with the caravan as far as Galway, and saying she had heard that they were traveling with that bloody-handed man, Robert the Englishman, and she wished to meet him, and how she would feel safe faring with such a one. . . ."

The color was rising in Nemain's cheeks. "And she with a cloud of gallowglasses about her, she needs my husband to feel safe? She should travel from town to town and tell stories for her bread. You see, Master Murchad, that a loose tongue is more dangerous than a bull that's out of the pasture."

Murchad reddened. "I pray you, forgive me, and, and, my tongue. 'Twas the drink, see you, and pride in your husband there."

The ale came, he drank it off, and with a mumbled farewell he went to sit by his uncle. Nemain gave a little snort of disapproval, and bent to wipe butter off the young queen's lips. Jack looked at Hob and Nemain, his eyebrows raised significantly, and Hob gave Jack a summary of what had happened, for Jack, whatever his other virtues, could not get Irish into his head.

BUT THEY SAW NOTHING of the gallowglasses nor of their fey queen that night. The Norse Gaels set up their tents in a corner of the big compound, as though on campaign, and Malmhìn slept within her travelling wagon, and food was brought out to them.

The next day the wagonmaster requested that the gallowglasses march in the vanguard, for "should any lurk within the greenwood, and they eyeing our wagons, and hungering for our goods, the sight of a battle of gallowglasses will spoil their appetite."

Molly remained within the wagon and Hob drove Milo from up on the seat, with his daughter beside him. From time to time the ox, so used to Hob walking beside him and in sight, looked around for him, Hob calling reassurance and encouragement.

Redmane, who had a grave manner and a serious disposition for one who was six years old, looked up at him and said, "Daddy, you treat Milo as if he were a baby!" She spoke in Irish, though half the time he and Nemain used English, so that she should know both, and now he was used to hearing "*a Dheaidí*" in Irish and "Daddy" in English.

"Well, treasure of my heart, he's big on the outside, but

he's just a wee fellow on the inside, and you see now, when he heard his name, and myself calling to him, how he turned back to the road. He just wants to know that all's well, for animals don't like changes from what they know." Hob found that speaking Irish to his daughter came more easily than speaking it to adults, perhaps because the concepts were simpler, or because he was more relaxed. Perhaps, he thought now, it's because she makes me so happy, and I don't think about what word to use.

She was watching Milo to see if he'd turn around again, and Hob was looking down at her pretty face, an echo of his beloved wife's. Nemain claimed to see Hob in the child's face, but Hob—less familiar with his face than Nemain was—could not. Macha was framed in her own red hair, blown forward like a flag on today's breezy afternoon, and Hob thought: This wondrous thing that has come into our lives: Macha Redmane!

"Jack treats Sweetlove like a baby, but she's just little," she said.

"Well, Milo's big, but he's still my baby. You're my baby, too."

Redmane drew herself up. "I am a queen."

And she was, or would be, thought Hob. Aloud he said, "You're my baby queen."

"I—"

"You're my queen baby."

"I—" She was starting to laugh, and before she could get the next word out, he said:

"You're the queen of the babies!"

"Da—"

"All the babies will crawl into your hall and say, 'Hail, O queen!' "

Macha Redmane was more like Molly than her mother, though she looked so much like Nemain. She was thoughtful and kind, where Nemain was mercurial and passionate and had a real temper. But Macha was still a child of six, and by now, under the barrage of Hob's teasing, she had dissolved into helpless laughter, which he suddenly caught from her, one setting the other off, a condition which Molly had called "the giggles," when he and Nemain, as children and beyond, had gotten into this state.

Hob was a man who could slaughter in one of his rages—Nemain had compared them in all seriousness to the *ríastrad*, the "distortion," the battle madness that came upon Cu Chulainn in the old tales. Hob was a man who had killed a giant, who had killed a wizard, who had killed a kind of demon, and yet . . . Having a child brought you back to being a child, thought Hob, wiping his eyes and sighing. Beside him, Redmane's mirth winding down, she sighed, almost a perfect echo and imitation of his own. They looked at one another then, and both went off into another gale of merriment, until Hob's side began to ache.

And then beyond her was a shadow, a sudden movement, and his hand went to the dagger at his hip, and there, a foot in the rope loop and one hand clinging to the bottom of the lantern mount, was the young queen, Malmhìn of the Uí Bháis, clad in a long shift of the coarse cloth called russet, ragged at the hemline. She hung there, swaying with the wagon's motion, agile and athletic, sun-darkened, her hazel eyes burning into his, her auburn hair uncovered, a massy tangle that hung down her back.

"Robert the Englishman," she said in a low, blurry voice; she spoke Irish with a strange accent, somewhat guttural. She was peering at him with a smoldering intensity. He could smell a musk coming off her, and her body was straining at the red cloth, and to his dismay he felt his body responding, a surge of lust washing over him.

Malmhìn looked at Redmane, then turned her eyes back on Hob; a moment later, as if troubled, she flicked a glance at the child again, but only for a moment. "The great killer! You have slain those many pirates, with this hand?" She was looking at his hand, still on the dagger hilt, and he took it away from the weapon, and rested it on his thigh. "And you have cleansed all that blood from it?"

She is touched or simple, thought Hob, and just then she leaned across Redmane and seized his hand, bending to it, and licked along his palm.

He was so astonished that he did nothing for a heartbeat, but his palm was tingling with the tactile memory of that rasping tongue, and there was a sensation of heat, as though he had spilled hot water on his hand.

Redmane sat up straight, and onto her delicate features came an expression he knew so well from Nemain's face, a flared-nostril lowered-eyebrow anger, and she said as coldly as an adult, "Do not do that."

The feral queen released Hob and her hand hovered before Redmane as though preparing a slap. Hob moved his feet under him and his hand went back to the leather-wrapped dagger hilt. I'll kill her here if she touches the child, he thought, and Jack and I will deal with the gallowglasses as we must.

She saw something of this in his change of stance, and she dropped her hand and smiled at Macha, a smile meant to be sweet, but with something ugly beneath. "This is your daughter? She is as fierce as her father, then." She looked closely at her. "Have you been in the West, then? Surely I have seen her before. . . ."

"Nay, Mistress, we are poor travelers new come to Erin."

Malmhìn swung back and forth a bit as she hung from the side of the wagon, as though playing a climbing game. Then: "Come to the tents of the gallowglasses tonight, Robert the Englishman, bloody-handed Robert, and I will give you dinner. Are you not hungry? I am hungry; I am always hungry. Put the child to bed tonight, and come have your meat with me."

Hob was unsure, now that all immediate danger to Redmane seemed to have passed, whether it was wise to antagonize this madwoman before Molly was ready for the coming war, but he had no intention of going to the gallowglasses' tents.

"Perhaps some other night, Mistress," he managed to say. He was acutely uncomfortable, poised between his daughter and a flood of desire that was roaring in his veins, a violent reaction to this woman's presence that he fought to conceal from Redmane; it was like a loud sound in his ears, making thought difficult.

"I am hungry, Robert Blood-hand. If you do not come, I will seek someone else."

Abruptly she dropped off the wagon and ran, not back up the line to where her escort of gallowglasses marched, but off into the woods, disappearing swiftly between the tree trunks. Hob caught the flash of her bare soles as she ran. A barefoot queen, he thought, and mad as the Gadarene swine.

"I don't like her," said Macha Redmane. She took his hand and felt his palm where Malmhìn had touched him. She got that faraway stiff-faced expression that Molly got when seeing what was not there, but what was to be. "Do you know, Daddy," she said in the voice of one half-asleep, "I think that Mommy is going to kill her."

WHEN THEY WERE CAMPED that night in another of the Tribes' caravanserais, and all in the big wagon, and Hob and Redmane telling of the strange visit of the youngest queen of the Uí Bháis, Molly fetched a clean cloth and soaked part of it in the *uisce beatha* and scrubbed his palm with it, muttering Irish prayers under her breath. Then she gave the cloth to Jack and told him to go outside and throw it in one of the cookfires.

"For there's no telling what an evil person with a touch of the Art may leave behind with so intimate an act," she said.

"She thinks she has seen Macha before," said Hob.

"It's unsure I am that she's able to think in a straight line," said Molly. "She's not a lackwit, but her thoughts are tangled, and it comes to me that she's remembering Nemain as she was as a child, and Macha resembling her mother as she does."

"I believe I am going to kill her," said Nemain.

Hob looked at Redmane.

"So I have heard," he said.

Chapter 8

MALMHÌN DID NOT COME BY THEIR wagons again, for which Hob was grateful, but they heard various stories of her strange behavior at other stops along the way, from wagon drivers who had observed her when the animals were being watered, or relayed by Adam or Murchad at the evening meals. She was seen wandering out at night, leaving by the inn door and entering the woods, coming back late and demanding admission through the postern gate in the innyard wall; at another stop she was discovered asleep outside the inn door at daybreak, curled up like a cat on the threshold. On one occasion, after sundown, the wagonmaster had had a question for the young queen; the sub-constable of her gallowglass contingent had admitted that he did not know where she went, "nor would I presume to ask her."

Molly, meanwhile, was chafing at having to stay hidden in the wagon, her meals brought to her. At night she would put on a heavy shawl and veil and walk about a bit near the wagons. There were only six more days of travel before they came into Galway, and there the troupe would part company with the merchants' caravan. The Benedictine priory guesthouse, where it had been arranged for them to stay by Monsignor da Panzano's agents, was not far.

The inns maintained along their trade road by the Tribes of Galway had their own permanent guards, who patrolled the oversized innyards to foil any attempts at theft by stealth. There were men stationed at the outer door of the inn proper, at the big gates into the innyard, and along the palisade walls, on walkways that ran around the inside, of a height that they could see—and shoot, if it came to that—outside, into the road and the surrounding terrain. The inn's guard enabled the road escort of mounted Irish kerns to stand down in the evenings once all wagons were secure within the innyard.

Hob awoke one morning to the sounds of some disturbance outside. Loud voices, angry voices. He could not determine the subject, but the hum and rumble of conversation swelled and subsided and swelled again. Plainly something was amiss. He dressed hastily and left Nemain stretching and yawning. He swung down from the wagon and made his way to the knot of men standing by the wooden palisade, on the side farthest from the inn itself.

He pushed through and stopped: there against the fence, naked, was one of the night guards, his throat sliced neatly through. He had been castrated, and mutilated in various inventive ways, apparently with the same very sharp blade that had severed much of his neck.

"Saint Michael protect us!" said Hob. "Has there been an attack?"

The innkeeper, Master Patrick, turned to him. "Nay, Master Robert, he was killed in secret last night, and there was no alarm, and no sign of a fight, and we're thinking 'twas an evil spirit, or one of the fairy folk. His clothes are over there, and he took them off by himself, so 'twould appear."

He indicated a pile of clothing by the fence, perhaps two yards away; from beneath the pile peeped the toes of the guard's boots, and crossed atop the pile were his dagger and truncheon. Master Patrick indicated his chief of guards. "And Matthew here says none of his comrades report hearing a thing."

Hob looked keenly at the ground around the corpse, but whatever tracks had been made, by victim or killer, had been obscured, either by the murderer last night or by this morning's crowd of onlookers.

He went back to the wagons and reported to Molly, wording it as discreetly as possible for the child's sake, what he had seen. They were in the large wagon with the others. Macha had fallen and skinned her knee; Molly was rubbing a salve gently into the abrasion.

The little girl was being stoic: "A queen must not cry, Daddy." Her lower lip was quivering a bit, though. Nemain sat beside her with her arm about her shoulders. Hob leaned against a chest and watched Molly's deft hands. Jack was on one elbow on the bed, a hand like a bear's paw gently ruffling the fur on Sweetlove's chest, the small dog lying on her back with an expression of glazed bliss.

In a little while the caravan would have a light meal in the inn's common room, and then take the road. Molly wrapped a linen strip around the knee and stood up, putting the stopper in the crock of salve, wiping her hands.

"And why, I'm thinking, would a strapping young guard be taking off all his clothes before an enemy, and he piling them neatly by the fence, and his weapons as well?"

"Because he's seeing no enemy near," said Nemain, "but only a friend."

"A friend?" said Hob. The women seemed to be speaking a secret language, and he felt himself a step behind. They were speaking in English, as a courtesy to Jack, but when Hob looked a question at him he just shrugged.

"A woman friend," said Nemain viciously. "I'm thinking it's that strange creature, who walks by night and all around."

"Malmhìn? But why would she kill him—surely he was not known to her. And, and why would she do . . . the rest?" said Hob, unwilling to go into detail in front of the child.

"Her heart is tangled," said Molly. "What should be straight is knotted, and love and blood-love are mingled within her. Those three queens are evil chieftains of an evil tribe, and she not least of them. She has spent too much time in the greenwood, and something of the shadows beneath the trees has come into her heart, and that something has a fanged soul."

BUT WHEN THE TROUPE, without Molly, who remained behind in the wagon, came into the inn's common room they found that all talk was of the murder, and that the gallowglasses had struck their tents at first light, hitched up their queen's travelling wagon, and marched away without waiting for the rest of the caravan. Common-room gossip seemed ready to fix suspicion on the gallowglasses and their strange young charge, especially since they seemed to have taken flight.

"They will never bring her to justice, away there in their ring fort that was ours, surrounded by those mailed men and their axes," said Nemain angrily. "But we will bring them all to justice, all of them, the red-handed spalpeens!"

Chapter 9

ANOTHER DAY'S JOURNEY, PLEASantly uneventful, brought the caravan to another haven of the Tribes of Galway. These inns are strung out, one day's journey apart, thought Hob, like the beads of a paternoster.

The merchants, the drivers, the caravan guards, and Molly's people filled the benches in the common room. Haunches of venison were roasting on iron spits in the great fireplace; bowls of stew, with beef, turnips, carrots, wild garlic, as well as trays of pork sausage, were set out down the middle of the long trestle table; stacks of dry oaten cakes were set between every two diners. The innkeeper, a tall man who, despite a broken nose and a turn in one eye, managed to maintain a surprisingly jovial expression, stood by the arch to the kitchen, gossiping with the wagonmaster.

At some point, the innkeeper had mentioned that a gallowglass contingent, with a luxurious travelling wagon, had passed the inn without stopping. At once a storm of questions was shouted at him from the merchants. Everyone was leaving his seat and clustering around him, clamoring for more information. Had the gallowglasses said anything? Had he seen the young queen within her travelling wagon? Had they threatened him in any way?

Surprised and dismayed, the innkeeper replied, "Nay, nay. They went past with that fast march-step they have, and the wagon closed and curtained as it was. Behind them came the squires with their javelins, but none even looked aside. 'Twas late in the afternoon, as well, and I thought they'd turn in at the innyard gate, but no, on they went, and soon we could no longer hear them. Perhaps they camped in a field—who would bother them?" He looked from one intent face to another. "But what has happened?"

Molly and her people were following all this closely. "She is trying to put at least a day's march between herself and this caravan, with its suspicion of her as a murderer and worse," said Molly.

"Surely this is not the first time she has done this," said Hob.

"Nay," said Molly. " 'Twas so smoothly accomplished—and 'tis the sort of thing she might, for safety, practice first close to home, and her sisters, and her tribe of axmen. I'm destroyed with worry for my people, with these blood-crazed foreigners controlling them, the farmers and their families, our great warriors dead or scattered. What will we find when we come to our home? This one, with her lust all knotted up with bloodletting, and the eldest, with her blood sorceries—what have they been doing to my kin?"

Abruptly she threw down the oat-cake she had in her hand and left the common room. Jack got up quietly and went out after her.

"As we're coming closer to the return, Herself is fretting," said Nemain. "She's torn between a burning to get on with it, and a fear of making a misstep, and so losing all."

"I've never yet seen her be uncertain; perhaps a little, when she faced all those sorcerous hyenas. . . ."

"She will prevail," said Nemain quietly. "You know she will."

WHEN THEY'D FINISHED EATING and went out into the inn-yard where the wagons were set against the wall, the soft summer night of Ireland had settled down. There was a high-pitched torrent of sound from the chorus of insects in the forest and in the meadows outside the palisade walls, and beneath that a sweet quiet stream of plucked notes: Molly's *claírseach*, coming from behind the mostly closed shutters on the big wagon. She was playing a piece in a minor key, somber, with the typical Irish plunge in pitch at the end of the last line.

"You will sleep with us tonight, beat of my heart," said Nemain, taking Redmane's hand and leading her toward the midsized wagon. She drew a key from her pouch and handed it to Hob: "Jack will be in there comforting Herself; go bring Sweetlove from the small wagon."

"If she'll deign to come with me," said Hob, "since I'm not Jack."

"And don't forget her water bowl," said Nemain. To Redmane she said, "Husbands: you must remind them of everything; they'd forget their heads were they not nailed on."

Hob was grinning as he trudged toward the little wagon; he could still hear the child's laughter as he reached the back door, and behind it the harp, and behind that the shrilling of thousands of courting insects. A peaceful night—he paused with his hand on the lock, and looked around carefully. The lanterns hung from the palisade walls, the bonfires here and there maintained by the inn's guards, the spill of light from the torches over the gate—all showed a scene of peace. Guards moved up on the wooden wall-walks; grooms came and went from the stables; a serving-man carried water from the innyard well, a yoke across his shoulders supporting two wood-stave buckets. Yet the last inn had been like this one, and a man had been butchered with no one the wiser.

Suddenly he was eager to get back to the wagon with his wife, his daughter, all that made his life precious. He turned the key in the iron cylinder, and opened the door—the interior was like a black cave, the light from the yard hardly penetrating. From within came a hair-raising low growl, the death-threat of a savage deep-forest killer.

"Oh, give over, you little sausage," said Hob, and here, emerging from the shadows, was Sweetlove, who had the grace to look somewhat sheepish. He took her up one-handed and put her down by his feet. He reached in and got her water bowl, tossed its contents into the dust of the innyard, and placed it on the wagon's apron. When he had the door closed and locked, he picked the dog up again and returned to his little family.

They settled down. Hob filled the dog's bowl from the water jug and put down the meal scraps they had brought from the common room. Nemain got into bed with Redmane, and began a nighttime story by the light of the candle on the chest by the bed. Hob got in under the thin summer cover, and the child, safe between them, was yawning and fighting to stay awake.

Sweetlove had finished her dinner and had a noisy drink, and now began to pace back and forth, whining softly for Jack, until Macha Redmane sat up and clapped twice. The little dog stopped and looked at her; the child patted the bed, and Sweetlove jumped up and settled at Redmane's feet.

"We will need a bigger bed, wife," said Hob, laughing. He lay back and listened to his beloved's voice as she resumed her narrative. Nemain had a delicate precise pronunciation when telling the old stories, and although an archaic term here and there eluded Hob's Irish, he was enjoying the tale: a fated king and his entourage were journeying toward a hostel run by a being called The Red God, the warriors a handsome sight with their ivory-hilted swords and silver shields; they rode beautiful high-spirited dapple-gray horses, horses with small heads and sharp ears, with broad hooves and large nostrils, with bridles of colored enamel.

He was drifting away with these pictures moving somewhere behind his eyes, when he became aware that silence had fallen, and Nemain was patting his shoulder. "Snuff the candle, my heart's treasure," she said, and so he did.

Chapter 10

The extent of Malmhìn's malevolence was revealed at the next way station, for as Molly said, "She could have murdered her way across Erin without attacking the outposts of the Tribes of Galway, yet she haunts these stations. Is it because you are following this path, Hob, and she desires to find you, or because you have refused her, and she wishes to frighten you?"

They had traveled peacefully from Colm's Inn—he of the broken nose—to the Widow Margaret's Inn, and stayed here with no indication of anything untoward, and this morning had arisen to another clamor, another corpse. Molly had at once suggested to the wagonmaster that he detach a couple of fast riders and send them on ahead to warn the other stations down the line, for it was obvious that she was going to repeat her predations, and the Tribes' caravanserais seemed to be her choice of hunting ground.

They left Redmane in the big wagon with Sweetlove, and went to inspect the killing. Once again the guard's clothes were removed with no sign of struggle. This time they were not folded into a stack, but they were in a heap, a few feet from the body; this man was perhaps not as habitually neat as his colleague. The corpse lay on its back in a puddle of gore: the throat was cut, there were deep slashes in the torso, and the genitals were missing entirely. Molly went over the body closely, as did Nemain—at one point each woman took one of the dead man's hands and held it for a moment, her eyes closed, trying to sense what had happened.

"We know, of course, 'twas her, Malmhìn—who else could charm a man out of his clothes, who else is strange enough to carve him like a side of mutton?" said Molly. "But 'twould be well to know just how she does it. There is not the residue of the Art, but there is a . . . tang that lingers, a scent as of a wodewose."

"Aye," said Nemain. " 'Tis the scent of her, surely, faint though it is."

Hob could detect nothing, although he did not doubt the women, whose senses were tuned to an exquisite pitch. But he remembered Malmhìn's scent, strong as a woodland animal; it had affected him on some primitive level, the signal from a female animal to the male, and even remembering it now he felt himself stirring. He resumed his inspection of the corpse, to distract himself from his thoughts.

"He had spent before he died," said Nemain, squatting

beside the dead guard. She pointed to the inside of his right knee, where a dried spatter glinted with pearl in the light of morning.

Hob was looking at a trail of red that ran from between the man's legs to a point perhaps five feet away. "But how comes this—yon blood trail runs *up* this little slope in the ground."

One of the mounted escorts, Liam, stood by, leaning on his lance as on a walking stick. "Sure, he's after being dragged over forninst the fence, but why?"

"He's not been dragged," said Molly, "or there'd be blood everywhere, not just in this one track up between his legs."

The little crowd—Molly and her people, a few of the horse guards, the inn's guards, and the wagonmaster—was silent for a while, contemplating the scene. The guards in particular were dismayed and angry; the inn guards at their colleague's death, the horse guards because in traveling constantly to and from Dublin, everyone knew everyone else by now.

Jack, that old campaigner, had been down on one knee, examining the ghastly remains—as a former mercenary, he had seen far worse. Now he stood.

"Lurgh," he said. Look.

He went to stand beside where the blood trail started. He put a hand between his legs, miming shock, and staggered back several feet, legs wide, then fell backward. He was lying next to the body, just outside the welter of blood. Blood spraying from between his legs would have produced a trail of red like the one leading to the dead guard.

"Och, aye, that's how it happened," said Molly. "And we may imagine what was happening a moment before."

Jack rolled up easily to his feet and Hob dusted him off.

"God as my witness, I'll be putting a dart into that bitch should we see her, queen or no queen," Liam muttered, to no one in particular. He straightened and, with an abrupt angry movement, shouldered his lance, spat aside into the dirt, and walked away.

The captain of the inn guards was one of those nearby. Molly said to him, "Have guards near, but not too near, each other. Have them keep one another in sight at all times. An alarm to be sounded on a horn if anyone sees her."

"Perhaps also have women keep watch with the men," said Nemain. "If nothing else, they may be able to give the alarm without falling beneath her spell."

Hob was walking around, looking in a widening spiral. Now he stopped. "But what *did* happen to his tarse, his stones?" he said.

"Better not to ask," said Nemain darkly. She licked her lips, and pretended to pat at her mouth with an imaginary cloth.

"She, she—Jesus be my savior!" cried Hob. "Can such things be?" But Hob had seen Sir Tarquin and his predations on Sir Odinell's peasantry, and he did not really doubt that Malmhìn had eaten of the guard's body; it was just that he had not lost his ability to be appalled.

Molly looked up over the palisade fence, to the wall of forest that began behind the innyard. "She moves through the forest like a cat; she climbs like a cat; like a cat, she must have her meat. Till we come within the walls of Castle Dunlevin, do not let Macha Redmane from your sight." She turned to Hob and Jack. "And you two, stay near Nemain or myself—with this one, 'tis the men that are weak and she that is strong."

Nemain turned abruptly and headed toward the wagons, where Redmane waited with Sweetlove. Hob crossed himself and went to follow her, walking slowly, lost in his thoughts.

He was remembering Malmhìn swinging like a child from the side of the wagon. He could hear her saying, "I am hungry; I am always hungry. Put the child to bed tonight, and come have your meat with me." Had he gone to the tents of the gallowglasses that night, would he have ended like that wretched thing back by the fence?

And he wondered also if Macha Redmane, daughter and granddaughter and great-granddaughter of adepts and priestesses of the Mórrígan, had, even at her tender age, sensed that she had to protect him from this woman, who sang the song that only men can hear, the song ancient as the bones of the earth, that overthrows their reason. The child had been instantly hostile to the Hebridean queen, and Malmhìn had reacted to this hostility with the quick anger of a predator interfered with on the hunt, and that had triggered Hob's protective reaction for his child. Hob did not think that Macha Redmane had known what she was doing or why, but he did think perhaps her instincts were more than those of a child.

And here was the large wagon. He put a foot in the rope

loop, swung up and opened the door, and there was his wife sitting on the bed, the child on her lap. Sweetlove jumped to her feet when Hob appeared, but seeing that it was not Jack, threw herself down again with a pronounced sigh that somehow seemed to convey a vexed disappointment. Hob sat beside his wife and child and put his arms around both of them and held them. He sat that way for a fair while, till Sweetlove jumped up with a *yip*.

A moment later he heard muffled speech, and then the wagon rocked as someone climbed to the tailboard. Molly entered, and Sweetlove did a little dance till she could get round Molly, and then she sprang into Jack's arms.

"Well, the Widow Margaret has her men and women readying that poor wight for burial," announced Molly. "And the caravan's preparing to move on, so it's on to the stables and see if Milo's willing to work today. Away on!"

Chapter 11

FOR THE WAGONMASTER, THE MERchants, the guards of the Tribes of Galway caravan, there was now fear that the young Hebridean queen—for all agreed that it was she behind the attacks—would strike again. Molly had an additional concern.

"If 'tis true that she's stalking us, her gallowglass escort staying ahead of us and herself slipping through the woods all unseen, and spying upon us, and biding her time for the next murder to slake her hunger, then I must continue to skulk within yon wagon. For 'twould be disaster should she recognize me and send warning to her sisters that we have returned."

She continued to ride in the wagon, or on occasion to sit on the wagon seat heavily veiled. But most of the time Hob drove the big wagon, his daughter on the seat beside him and Milo looking around every so often for reassurance. Despite the sense of menace the events of the last week or so had engendered, Hob felt his spirits lifting. They were now more than two-thirds of their way across Ireland, Milo's inexorable tread carrying them nearer with every day to the sea, to their rendezvous with the Normans, and to the final preparations for revenge.

And the journeying was physically pleasant: the scouts employed by the Tribes of Galway skirted the worst of the bogs, and their road lay through thick forest loud with birdsong: robins sang chirruping warnings that the wagons were invading their territory, a sound complemented by the chaffinches with their *fink!* and wrens with their warbles that ended in a low buzz. In the foreground was the drowsy hypnotic rumble and creak of many wagon wheels, the thud on the earth of Milo's big cloven hooves. The air was cool in the shade of the forest trees, the leafy branches overhanging the trail like a partial roof.

A fox, followed by two half-grown kits, loped across the trail in the interval between the wagon ahead and Molly's wagon. The second kit paused midway and froze, transfixed by the sight of the oncoming ox; from the brush came a sharp bark, a command; the kit awoke with a start and completed its dash across the trail, causing Redmane to cry out with glee as it dove into the grass just ahead of Milo's hoof.

Red deer appeared and vanished in the spaces between the trees some little distance into the forest—beyond that, shadow and the overlap of tree trunks made them invisible. Hob told stories and tried to answer the scores of questions the child asked about the birds, the trees, the sky.

Periodically scouts, in pairs or singly, rode back along one side of the caravan, making sure that all were accounted for; this also ensured that there were guards within hail all along the length of the convoy. Since the attack, Jack was now driving the rearmost wagon, and so after a horse guard came cantering down past them, a moment later he'd come riding up on the other side.

One such rider rode back past them, circled Jack's tailboard, and rode, pushing his horse, back up toward the head of the column. But a few wagons ahead he slowed to a walk, and turned his mount aside into the forest. When they came up to where he'd turned off, his horse was standing patiently, its reins loosely twirled about a stiff outlying branch of a blackthorn shrub; its rider, back to the trail, was making water by a tree.

They were past in a moment, and rumbling along, Hob deep in a story about a princess and a giant, when the scout jogged past them and headed back up the line.

When, several miles later, they passed another horse by the side of the trail, its reins secured around the trunk of a birch sapling, Hob thought nothing of it, and a short while later a guard rode past on that self-same horse, obviously having relieved himself.

Telling a story to Redmane involved a certain amount of work, and a certain amount of devotion to detail, for she wanted to know *everything* about what was happening. He was telling this story in English, because it was Macha's day to speak English.

"Then this giant—"

"Daddy, what was the giant's name?"

"His . . . name. His name was, was . . . Hugh. But his friends called him 'Tiny.' "

"But he was a giant. Why would they call him Tiny?"

"It was a jest among themselves, you see. He's very big, so they call him Tiny because the name fits him so badly."

"Oh. And then what happened?"

What a serious little person, thought Hob; Redmane was watching him intently, eager to hear the next turn of the tale. And he thought he would tell her about—

"Redmane, *a rún,* go in the wagon. Tell *sin-seanmháthair* to come out. Stay till I call you."

A good child, Macha Redmane: she knew when things had turned serious, and wasted no time with questions. She disappeared through the front hatch and a moment later he heard Molly going out the back door and climbing the rear rope ladder. She appeared above him, standing wide-legged at the leading edge of the roof, keeping her balance easily despite the movement of the wagon.

"Hob, lad, what's amiss?"

"There," said Hob, pointing forward. He had seen the signs of trouble far ahead, and wanted to get the child inside. Beside the trail was a cluster of horses, held by one of the guards, and he was sure there was some mischief under the trees. As the wagon came up to the scene, he was proved right: in under the roof of leaves, a handful of guards stood around a tiny clear space, and in the center was a corpse. Even from up on the wagon seat he could see that the man was naked. He halted Milo and set the brake. He swung down; behind him, he could hear Molly descending the front ladder.

The other two wagons behind him were stopping; Nemain and Jack were dismounting. They went in under the trees into an instant green twilight. The collapse of an old tree had taken three saplings with it; the result was this patch of open ground, the size of a very small room, with a border of wood avens, their bright yellow flowers spotted here and there in the dimness; the center of the clearing was a thick carpet of dark bluebells, and the scent arose of those crushed beneath the body and in what must have been a very brief, very violent struggle. The perfume of the flowers, so lovely in itself, did not mix well with the odors of blood and other substances produced by the corpse which, by virtue of the deep gashes in its torso, revealed its inmost secrets. Once again there was a hollow, a gore-filled portal, where should have been the genitals.

Hob forced himself to show no emotion. Jack was stolid as well, although Hob was sure that, after a life spent mostly in campaigning, Jack actually *was* unmoved in the face of such horrors. The two Irish queens, with their stern discipline and devotion to the Mórrígan, who after all was a war goddess, went briskly about examining the scene, and the unfortunate guard, for signs of Malmhìn: the wounds were made by very sharp steel, not by the teeth of wolf or bear; no one had heard the attack, which must have been a complete surprise to the victim, and the guard's clothes, his lance and other weapons, were a short distance away. He had been seduced and then, in midpassion or just afterward, had been butchered like a sheep.

Molly was doing a close examination of the slain guard. Again there were signs that the guard had spilled his seed, and again it was on himself and not within a partner, indicating that there was not a true coupling occurring at the moment he was slain.

"She's attending to him in some other way," said Molly, "and when she has him at his moment, and so at his most helpless, she strikes."

Hob went a bit beyond the clearing, walking bent over. Jack came beside him, and they looked for anything amiss. This was what was known in England as a bluebell wood, and the lovely flowers stretched, dense as carpet, in every direction. Here and there some were crushed—he indicated a patch where the plants were disturbed, some torn free of the earth. But Jack just shook his head and pointed to a pile of the dark pebble-like deer scat.

They moved slowly farther into the woods. Bees murmured among the dark bells of the flowers, and some little distance away they could hear Molly and Nemain commenting to each other in short muttered phrases. The wind moved the thick roof of leaves above them, producing a moaning rustle, and the women's voices were hidden beneath it, and the road and the caravan seemed somehow much farther away.

All of a sudden Jack, with the keen senses that infused

his body even when not in the Beast state, threw up his head. He looked this way and that down the long dim aisles between the trees. Hob could not hear anything, but suddenly became aware that they were severed from the road by a perceptible distance. Formidable as they were, they had only their daggers.

The gloom beneath the tree canopy seemed to darken further, and the view between the tree trunks, like pillars in some strange church, became not only fainter, but seemed to grow in menace, as though the air were curdling, were thickening in preparation for some manifestation of a demon, or a malevolent woodland god.

Or, thought Hob, Malmhìn herself, with whatever unholy powers she possessed. Jack signaled that they should retreat, which they did, both men facing backward, so that they might not be rushed upon from behind, and they all unaware.

And then they were back by the clearing, and, with a last backward glance, rejoined the women and the guards and the wagonmaster, who by now, curious at the holdup, had come back down the line to investigate.

Hob and Jack stood off to one side. Hob, leaning close, said to Jack, speaking quietly, "Was there something back there?"

The man-at-arms nodded. He indicated the forest with a sweeping circular motion: *the woods.* "Whidgecraght," he gargled. Witchcraft. Hob looked back under the trees, at the shadows, the aisles between the tree trunks leading into darkness, into nothingness. Later, when he told Molly and

Nemain about it, Molly said, "She is a creature of woodland magic; her weapon is her body and she uses it against the men, but who knows what other creatures—a wolf pack, say—listen to her back there in the forest? Listen to her, and obey her."

Now Molly rose from her examination and came away from the body. She stooped and pulled wild mint from near the base of an oak and crushed a handful between her palms, laving her hands with it.

The wagonmaster turned his horse and trotted out of the clearing into the road; he wanted to get the caravan rolling again. The captain of the horse guards was issuing orders for the collection of the body and she went up to him, drawing a large hand-cloth from the recesses of her gown and wiping her hands dry.

"Be said by me," she said to him, "if your men have need to empty their bladders, do it by twos: one to watch, and turn by turn."

"'Tis joyful I'll be when we roll into the Tribes' compound in Galway; I'll face mortal enemies, but this death by ghost . . ." He wore two thin braids at his temples; one was weighted with a little wooden cross, the other, just to be careful, was Thor's hammer rendered in pewter, doubtless from one of the Ostmantown shops, with their Viking-descended shopkeepers. He had been playing with the hammer, rolling it between thumb and forefinger, and now he crossed himself.

"We're not far—another day and a half, is it, lad?" asked Molly.

The captain, a lad of perhaps thirty-five with three children of his own, nodded.

"Soonest begun, soonest done," said Molly, turning and heading back to the road. "Away on!"

The wagons ahead were beginning to move. Hob swung up into the driver's seat; Nemain and Jack headed for their wagons; Molly went to the back of the wagon and climbed in, slamming the door. A moment later the hatch opened and Molly handed her great-granddaughter out to Hob. He settled the child on the seat and picked up Milo's knotted reins from the notch in the footboard.

"Would you like to release the brake?" he asked her, knowing she liked to help with the driving.

She pulled it free and he called to Milo, and they were off.

"So then what did the giant do?" she asked.

Hoofbeats were coming up on the rear right, and he thought quickly. "Give Daddy a kiss first," he said.

She turned toward him and stretched her arms up around his neck and kissed his cheek, and he put his free arm around her and held her to him as the horse guards galloped past, going up the line with a riderless horse in the middle of their squad, a shapeless bundle draped across the saddle, tied at both ends, the ropes meeting beneath the horse's belly, the corpse swaddled in a thick white cloth swiftly turning sodden red.

The Irish guards' horses were trained to battle and

were unaffected by their ghastly burden, but Milo, sensitive pacific Milo, veered sharply leftward when the smell of so much blood reached his nostrils. Hob let Macha go and hauled Milo back to the center of the trail. The guards were safely up the line, where they'd transfer the corpse to a wagon for the rest of the sad journey.

Macha Redmane was looking at him, and he stared back for a moment at the impossibly delicate features, the open and heart-happy expression. She was kind and—for a six-year-old—even dignified; she was wonderfully intelligent. Malmhìn was someone's daughter, too, yet afflicted with a limited understanding, a tangled mind, and that mind mixed with a bestial lust to inflict pain and suffering. If she is anyone's daughter, thought Hob, she must be Satan's. How could these two daughters, these two lives, exist—so different, yet side by side at the same time, in the same forest?

"Daddy . . ."

He became aware that he was staring at her, lost in his thoughts, swaying to the wagon's motion.

"Yes, well, um, the giant—"

"Tiny."

"Yes, of course, Tiny. Well, the next day . . ."

Chapter 12

When at last Molly's family had parted ways with the merchants' caravan as it turned off for Galway town, Adam and Murchad urging them to come and enjoy their hospitality, and the thanks of the Tribes of Galway council for saving a valuable cargo, they made their way to the Benedictine priory of St. Mary's. The priory was within sight of Dunlevin Castle, where they would rendezvous with Sir Jehan and the other Normans who had, for love of and gratitude to Molly, agreed to go on campaign this year to reinstate Molly and Nemain in their ancestral home.

Molly had been careful to obtain agreements from all her allies that they would meet, more or less within a specified week, at the castle, and that a place to stay themselves for a few days, and to board the animals—for however useful the three draft beasts were, they were no help in battle—would be available at the priory. She did not want to stay at the castle until the last moment, for the Normans would be arriving by separate ships, and debarking, and getting themselves established, and if the Uí Bháis had spies along this coast, she did not want them seeing the queen of the Ó Cearbhaills joining a Norman war party.

Eventually, of course, Molly's family would move to the castle, but if they could gain even one more day's anonymity by staying at the priory, it might be the difference between surprising their enemies and having their enemies all prepared and waiting for them.

At the priory they had been welcomed warmly by the prior himself, who, unsure of their connection, was yet pleased to accommodate honored friends of the papal legate Monsignor da Panzano—he had had a letter come by hand from Rome! Did they know Father Ugwistan, a Berber priest? Did they know that the holy Augustine was a Berber, and originally called Ugwistan?

Molly assured him that they knew Father Ugwistan, and Monsignor da Panzano, and had worked with them in England, although she was vague as to the nature of that work. The prior, a man of the far western edge of the known world, found their connection to Rome, the center of the Church, where St. Peter had walked and died, fascinating: he was certain they were persons of great moment in the halls of the Church. Hob thought it was amusing, and also rather touching.

In any event, the prior had settled them in a fairly spacious guesthouse, one of several maintained by the priory for pilgrims and visiting churchmen. Molly was pleased to find that the letter had been brought by Father Ugwistan, the Berber priest whose company she had enjoyed during her struggle against King John's sorcerer, and happy to find that he was well. The prior—one Patrick of Donegal—seemed confused by their plan to leave the three draft animals at the priory "until their transfer to our home can be arranged."

"Would you like the priory to purchase them from you?" asked Brother Patrick. "We have need of animals to pull the plow, and of course we have our own butchers if they should prove unsuitable for work."

At this Hob's face darkened and he took a step forward. His expression was so dire that the prior took a step backward, and Molly put out a swift hand to take him by the elbow. But when Hob spoke, his deep bass took on so melodious a tone that it was almost a lullaby; yet this somehow made it more, rather than less, menacing.

"I would have you treat them with all care, even as though they were members of your community, and if you return them to us in good condition when we are ready for them, the priory will be well rewarded. They have served us well for many years, and—" Hob was trying to remember a Bible verse that old Father Athelstan would quote to him as a boy. "Does not the scripture say that the laborer should have his wage, and the ox that treads out the grain should be allowed to eat some of it?"

The prior was uncertain what he had done to anger Hob, but he found this large man looming over him frightening, although he could not say precisely why—Hob had made no threats, and spoke only in that polite caressing voice that accorded so ill with his ferocious facial expression.

"I'm sure we can do what is needful for any friend of Monsignor da Panzano's, and he speaks highly of Mistress Molly, and we have brothers who are skilled in caring for our horses and oxen, and, and, in short, we shall treat them well till you can reclaim them." He was speaking rapidly, but keeping an eye on Molly's restraining hand, lest she lose her mollifying influence on this menacing stranger.

But Hob just bowed, and said, "Then I am sure we will be the best of friends, and that our people will ever be well-disposed toward St. Mary's."

When Molly and her family had departed to pen the beasts and to find supper, Prior Patrick drew a cloth from his sleeve and wiped his brow, which he found to be quite damp.

It was dusk by the time they had stabled the beasts, fed and watered them, and sat to eat at the refectory among a handful of other travelers: pilgrims setting off on the long road to the Holy Land, a pair of merchants bound for Bantry in the south. They were given a corner to themselves, that they might be undisturbed, which suited Molly well, anxious as she was not to have their presence noted prematurely. The little distance from the other diners meant they could speak somewhat more freely.

The staff had evidently been told to pamper Molly's family; there was some confusion about whether they had come from Rome, where one or more of them worked for the Holy Father, or from England, where one of them owned a castle, or two castles. Molly maintained an enigmatic silence toward all hints, veiled queries, and the like. In the end, what was known about them by the staff was only that they were guests of Brother Prior, and important in some way.

Certainly the food was not stinted. They supped on oat bread, salmon and trout basted with honey and sprinkled with salt and cooked on spits, a carrot-and-onion stew thickened with seaweed; to drink they had wheat ale flavored with herbs. Macha Redmane was given buttermilk to drink, and a bowl of raspberries and cream for a treat.

"'Tis a fine table they're setting for us," said Molly, sitting back with that sigh that a pleasantly full stomach produces. She had eaten with her usual robust appetite; one of the Norse Gael gallowglasses would have found her portions satisfying.

Nemain began to laugh. "And we should be thankful they're feeding us at all, with Hob frightening that poor prior halfway to his death—I wish that you could have seen the look on you, husband, when he suggested eating Milo! 'Twas the face of death itself, and he only trying to help."

"Perhaps I was overharsh with our host," said Hob. "But think you, culver, he also spoke of Mavourneen, and had they not found a use for her, they might have sent her to their shambles, and what say you to that?"

Nemain had not, because of Hob's immediate protest at the prior's suggestion, given any extended and serious thought to the threat to their draft animals, especially her darling Mavourneen, the small strong velvet-nosed ass who had been her pet since childhood. Now her brows drew down, and her mouth formed into a thin line, and beneath her skin, the near-translucent skin of the red-haired, a flush of crimson crept up her throat. She opened her mouth to speak, but Hob forestalled her:

"Watch Mommy call vile curses down upon our host," he said to Macha Redmane, and Molly burst out laughing, and Nemain, only slightly embarrassed, relaxed into a slow grin, and swatted at Hob's arm. Macha, not certain of what was occurring, smiled because everyone was laughing. She was not the daintiest eater, and Nemain busied herself with removing a trail of cream that threatened to escape from the child's chin to her shift, and peace reasserted itself at their corner of the refectory.

Jack and Molly were settling themselves in one room of the guesthouse while Nemain was putting Redmane to bed in another, when Hob came back from the wagons, chocked against the inner wall of the priory, with a jug of barley beer. He went to the room Nemain and he were to use as a bedroom, and set the jug on a table against the wall. This close to the great Western Ocean, the perpetual sea breeze kept the days cool and the evenings chilly, and the priory servants had built a small fire in the hearth. The play of the flames, the crackling of the wood, spoke of refuge and ease after effort. Hob stretched, and rubbed his hands over his face. It had been a long trip with a great deal of walking, and he was bone tired.

Hob removed the belt from which was slung his sword and war dagger in their scabbards, rebuckled it, and looped it carelessly over a peg in the wall; he turned to the table against the wall and reached for the jug of barley beer. The scabbard gave a series of diminishing taps as it swung from the sword belt against the plaster, slowly coming to a rest, and Hob froze in the act of pulling the stopper: had he heard another sound beneath the tapping—a creak of wood, the groan of shutter hinges? To his nostrils came a rich and complex scent: woman's sweat, musk, spices, the suggestion of autumnal woodland. A chill coursed through him, and he whirled.

Malmhìn crouched beneath the window. She had trailed them here, Hob thought in confusion, but how? Perhaps keeping the caravan in sight, her gallowglasses sent ahead, and herself moving in parallel through the woodland beside the road? And now she had landed, light as a hunting cat, on two feet and one hand, and she straightened slowly and took a pace toward him. She wore a patchwork shift of small-animal skins, fur and leather stitched together like a quilt, and held closed with a complex arrangement of thongs, over a kilt of the same handiwork. She halted, head a bit lowered: she was of no great height, so that she regarded him with large hazel eyes turned up toward him from under strong brown gull-wing eyebrows. In the thick mane of auburn hair that fell to her waist she had twined a chaplet of oak leaves. Deep in her throat she made a low steady moan, a vibration, the sound of a large cat contemplating its prey.

She took two more steps toward him, and the sway of her hips, the straining of her body against its garments, the strong and womanly scent of her, left him dizzy with lust, his body treacherously reacting on its own. *Awake! Awake!* he cried within himself. *This is your death before you, coiled to strike!* But still he could only stand and stare; the male in him was snared by her body, fascinated into immobility as a rabbit before a snake.

She reached up and tugged upon a leather thong, and her shift fell open in front; her heavy breasts, tipped with dark brown areolas, oval in shape and slightly tilted, augmented the sense that she was some creature of the forest, very female but not quite human.

Now her purr slid up into speech: "Come to me, Robert the Englishman."

He was light-headed with desire, and was on the point of taking a step toward her—he felt that if he took that step he would be unable to turn back, and he stood rigid, trying to throw off this sweet powerful glamour that gripped him.

There had been a time—he just thirteen, Nemain just fourteen and no more to him than a sister—when she had broken into his mooncalf contemplation of the lovely Margery atte Well with a sardonic "Would you ever cease a moment from your fierce courting and cut us a bit of that meat?" The memory of that sharp-tongued little girl came to him now, and the incongruity of it contrasted with the sight of this woman, crouched before him like a panther in heat, wrenched a sharp bark of laughter from him.

And with that the spell snapped like a rotted string: Malmhìn was still a handsome woman, but Hob's head had cleared, and he took a step back, putting up his hands in a gesture of refusal.

She saw this and pulled another string and the kilt fell open; she bent and put her right hand between her strong smooth thighs.

"Nay, demoiselle," he said to slow her, to give himself time to reach his sword, "give over. It's that I am a marriage man." He knew as he said it that his Irish was slightly off, and he amended it: "A married man," and it was perhaps this that distracted him a bit so that when her hand came up from between her legs with a wicked little curved-blade knife he almost did not move quickly enough.

It took all the skill that Molly and Sir Balthasar had trained into him to keep him alive: Malmhìn was as fast as anyone he had seen, perhaps even faster than Sir Jehan, that paragon of martial speed. Hob threw himself back a pace, another, and the steel made a silver semicircle a finger's breadth in front of his throat.

The table was against his back now and her knife was coming around on the backstroke. He groped backward for his dagger, hanging from his belt on the wall, but it was far too late; he threw up his left arm and the little knife snagged on his sleeve. Something hissed in his ear, and a moment later Malmhìn staggered backward, a black-fletched arrow transfixing that graceful throat. She stood for a heartbeat, choking on her own blood, and then collapsed in a sprawl of limbs. She thrashed for a moment or two; gradually she grew still.

Nemain stalked from the dark doorway, bow in hand. She bent over the other woman, and watched for a moment to assure herself that Malmhìn was dead. She reached down and plucked the sickle-dagger from the still-clenched hand. She examined it closely.

"She has poisoned the tip," Nemain said. She tossed the knife into the blaze of the fireplace. "Are you cut at all?"

Hob looked at his left arm. He was unscathed, but there was a rent in the sleeve of his shirt. Around the ragged edge of the hole was a discoloration: a touch of amber, a gleam of moisture. He held it up to her.

"Stand still," she said, and carefully drew the shirt up over his head, and drew the sleeve from his arm with utmost care. She stepped to the hearth and threw the garment into the fire, stepping back quickly to avoid the smoke.

She turned to Hob and put a small hand to the back of his neck, pulling him down to her for a kiss. He put his arms around her and they stood like that for a while.

"My faithful Hob," she said. "Wasn't she a grand sorceress of the body now, and you standing firm against her." She grinned up at him. " 'I am a marriage man,' he says. Well, 'tis not how you said it, 'tis that you *did* say it."

Hob looked at her. "And had I *not* said it—?"

"Oh," she said sweetly, reaching over her shoulder and patting the quiver slung to her back, "I have other arrows."

Part II

THE MOTHER

Who is she that looketh forth as the morning,
faire as the moone, cleare as the sunne,
and terrible as an armie with banners?

—Song of Solomon 6:10

Chapter 13

MOLLY LOOKED DOWN THE LONG table, empty save for linen cloths, beakers of wine and various drinking vessels, and a large parchment map unrolled and held open with a salt cellar, two empty goblets, and a scabbarded dagger. To her right sat Sir Maurice, one of the FitzAnthonys, whose castle this was; to her left was Sir Jehan. They were in an upper room, and through the open windows drifted the sweet smell of growing things, the scent of green Erin, mixed with the bracing salt-and-iodine tang of the Western Ocean, that began not far away and ran to the world's edge.

Hob was down the table on Molly's right, seated after Nemain and before Jack. There was a rustle and a sigh from under the table; Hob looked down and saw Sweetlove, inevitably following Jack around, just settling herself, her muzzle pillowed on the big man's shoe. Across the table, on Sir Jehan's left hand, loomed the glowering bulk of Sir Balthasar, the castellan and mareschal of Sir Jehan's Castle Blanchefontaine. Next sat two of Molly's own clan, the smith Bróccan and Daire, a sandy-haired, well-knit man in perhaps his early thirties, one of the few members of Molly's household guards to escape the slaughter by the Uí Bháis. Away on a hunting trip, he had returned to find his family murdered and the remnants of the clan reduced to serfdom by the outlanders. He had promptly gone into exile and, after some difficulty, succeeded in contacting Bróccan where the smith had come to refuge in Dublin.

Now Bróccan had left his wife and young son in charge of the forge; the journeymen and apprentices could keep the simpler affairs of the smithy going until Bróccan should regain his family's lands, or gain his death facing the Hebridean axes. The Norman knights had come with their retinues by coaster around the south of Erin, to the mouth of the river Shannon, and landed their horses and supply wains and grooms and men-at-arms and marched to this castle, to settle in and wait for Queen Maeve's arrival.

The levy from Castle Blanchefontaine was twenty-one knights; nine were Blanchefontaine household knights and twelve were Sir Jehan's vassals. With them Sir Jehan had mustered fifty-six men-at-arms from villages that owed him service. Sir Odinell, with his greater estates, had brought thirty knights and eighty-one men-at-arms. Molly had managed to collect, by secret messengers throughout much of Erin, almost a hundred of her scattered tribesmen who had avoided the virtual enslavement imposed on most of the free farmers of the Ó Cearbhaills. These had managed to flee the Uí Bháis and scatter with their wives and children across the land, finding refuge among distant relatives, or sympathetic tribes resentful of all foreign invaders. Now the men had returned, bearing the usual arms of Irish kerns: a pair of javelins, a single-handed ax, and a dagger. They were hardy fleet-footed men; they went barelegged and barefoot, and could launch a fierce swift attack and then be gone in an instant, melting away into the forest.

Now Molly rose and ran a finger along the crudely drawn map, with its stylized mountains and roads indicated by two parallel lines; the left edge was mostly a blank, broken here and there by the triple sinuous lines that represented waves: the Western Ocean.

"When we move, 'tis necessary that we move at speed; if we can come to this meadow and establish ourselves on this hillside, and muster into your battle formation"—here she nodded at Sir Jehan, who was acting commander of the Norman contingent—"before they are able to block the roads, 'twill give your great horses a clear field for a charge."

"We will sweep them into the sea," said Sir Odinell.

"These are gallowglasses from the Western Isles, and renegades to boot," said Sir Jehan. Eternally restless, he was moving his goblet and the wine jug beyond it with his left hand, lining them up, one in front of the other, then setting them side by side. Most of his right hand had been lost on Fox Night; he wore a beautifully sculpted bronze hand within which his maimed hand fit as though in a glove, the legend *Cave Sinistram,* "Beware the Left Hand," graven just behind the knuckles, and picked out in green gold. "You must not . . . not underestimate them, brother; they can put up a shield-wall"—he paused to turn the goblet about on its stem—"a shield wall with staked lances and they are . . . well-covered in mail, made with all the craft of the old Northmen—and a padded gambeson beneath that. They are skilled—skilled!—in strife from boyhood, and do not surrender easily."

"They are evil men," said Molly, "but they are not white-livered atall; they are hard to kill."

Sir Balthasar had said nothing to this point; the great killer of the North Country and Sir Jehan's chief enforcer against the Scots and their cross-border raids, he was both powerful of body and proficient at slaughter, with weapons or without. Now he stood and, from a sack of coarse cloth, produced a long-handled horseman's ax with a drooping bearded blade on one side and a straight spike on the other.

"Mail such as theirs is not easily broached," he said in the grinding bass that was, for him, a pleasant conversational tone. "I have had old Thierry and his men produce several score of these; they worked all last winter to accomplish that. Every knight will have one to hang from his saddle. The pick will find its way through the links; if not, the ax will break the foeman's ribs."

Molly took up the weapon and examined it; she was a strong woman and she brandished it one-handed to get the feel of it. "'Tis well—I'd like one as well, if you please."

Sir Balthasar bowed. "My lady."

"Sir Jehan, you have established your order of battle?"

But Sir Jehan could sit still no longer. He arose and paced as he spoke. "We will divide into . . . into three companies of knights. I will command the center; Sir Odinell will command the left wing, and Sir Balthasar the right. Young Giant's-bane here will ride with Sir Balthasar. He will want to observe his mentor in"—he paused, spun on his heel, and paced back—"in a fixed battle, of which he has not had experience before."

Hob had killed a seven-foot-tall knight, climbing him like a tree and putting a dagger into his eye, and so the Normans often referred to him as "Giant's-bane."

"There's a mort of pirates rotting on the floor of the Irish Sea who'd be sore astonished to hear how inexperienced at battle he is," said Nemain with the sharp-as-vinegar tone she used when annoyed.

Sir Jehan bowed to her; opened his mouth to reply; thought better of it; and simply nodded.

"'Twill be another week before we're ready to march, with our kinsmen still trickling in as they are," Molly said. "Daire will command the kerns. These gallowglasses are so heavily armored, 'twill be best if your knights deal with them direct. It's used to fighting in linen that my people are, not in steel, and these Scots have the advantage of them. I'm thinking that I'll give you my tribesmen as skirmishers and harriers, and let you order your own folk. How say you to this, Sir Jehan?"

"You have the right of it, Madam. If we can reach open ground—open ground on a rise, if possible—and set ourselves for battle before these Norse Gaels attack, I'd want the kerns as flanking skirmishers, hurling . . . hurling their javelins at the enemy's sides, falling back to our right and left flanks when the enemy counterattacks: we do not want them standing toe to toe with ironclad gallowglasses. We will leave gaps . . . aisles, if you will . . . in the ranks of our massed knights. Our men-at-arms can harry the gallowglass flanks if they charge."

He sat down again, and began clinking his metal hand against the side of his goblet, very softly. The others, used to his fidgets, ignored this. The energy that thrummed through Sir Jehan's bones and made him so unquiet also made him vibrant and athletic, and one of the fastest swordsmen in England, even with his left hand. "The while your kerns are darting in upon the Uí Bháis from the side, our Welsh archers will stand . . . stand before us and fire into the Hebrideans. Again, should they counterattack, the archers will run back through the channels left open for them by the knights."

" 'Tis well," said Molly. "Two more words for you: each gallowglass has two squires, as it were, and they attend him, and before the gallowglasses charge, these run out as skirmishers, and cast javelins, three to a squire, and so you must expect that, and be ready with your shields. The other word is that there are two of these evil queens left to us, and one a warrior queen and the other a fell sorceress. It's for that reason that I'll stay in reserve with Queen Nemain, and Jack as our personal guard, and we will watch for any least quiver of spellcraft, or deal with the warrior queen as may be needed."

"Our Welshmen will shred them to mince with their

longbows and their clothyard arrows," growled Sir Balthasar. "And your kerns may finish those who seek to flee."

"'Tis well," said Molly. "And now for supplies on the march. Sir Odinell?"

That knight was quartermaster for this expedition, and soon launched into a list of preparations made or to be made. Hob looked out the tower window, over the curtain wall, to the priory a quarter mile away. In the priory meadow, amid the monks' sheep, he could just make out the reclining form of Milo in the long green Irish grass, and beneath a solitary tree, the mare Tapaigh and the little ass Mavourneen, standing near each other, tails now and then flicking up over their hindquarters. How small they seemed, this far away; how far away that life, for the most part happy, traveling with Molly and Jack and Nemain as entertainers, as healers. It was in that priory that Hob had left off his old self, had said good-bye to Hob and resumed his identity as Sir Robert. As proud of his knightly spurs as he was, inevitably there was something lost in such a change in his life's position.

If we succeed in regaining our tribal lands, he thought, I will see to it that those three innocents will live out their lives in comfort, grazing peacefully till their old bones lie down for a long sleep.

The bailey at Dunlevin was ample, with a great expanse of level ground gone to grass. One of the Ó Cearbhaills' scattered tribesmen had taken the war chariot of the tribe's queens away with him when disaster struck, and brought it back with him when Molly's call to arms went out across Erin. When today's war council had concluded, Molly and Nemain had gone to the stables to fetch it. It was a two-wheeled wicker vehicle in an ancient style, with wooden cylinders attached, one on each side, to the outside of the chariot: each held several javelins. A warrior and her charioteer would keep their feet on the shifting, jouncing floor of the car, while one drove and the other hurled javelins or swung a sword as they flashed past an enemy. Molly's murdered daughter, Macha, had been her charioteer in the old days, and so she had thought she might have to forgo its use in the coming battle, and fight from horseback instead, but Nemain had taken so rapidly to the vehicle, that in the three weeks they had been here she had become almost as expert as her lost mother. Certainly she could keep her balance, drive well, and even hit the mark with a javelin while at full gallop.

Sir Fulk, Castle Dunlevin's mareschal, had provided two spirited mares to draw the war car, and as Nemain gained skill in driving them, the horses were learning what was expected of them, responding to verbal commands as well as the pull of the reins, working with each other on either side of the draw pole and not wasting time and effort by falling out of step.

Redmane and Sweetlove were waiting impatiently for their respective men when Hob and Jack stepped out onto the grass of the bailey: Redmane was swept up into a hug from her father and Sweetlove, after running full tilt around Jack, barking with a falsetto edge of hysteria, leaped up toward his chest, to be caught and held under one arm, where she subsided, giving every sign of contentment. Hob took Macha's hand and he and Jack strolled over to one side of the bailey, where several of the men-at-arms from Blanchefontaine and Chantemerle had gathered to view the afternoon's practice, the men squatting or sitting, backs braced against the curtain wall.

"Sir Robert! Giant's-bane!" called several in greeting; the men began to come to their feet in respect. Hob made a patting motion with one hand: *Sit, sit.* Here, from Castle Blanchefontaine, were the grizzled sergeant Ranulf and the man-at-arms Roger, now a sergeant as well. Hob had known them since he was a boy. They sat back, and made a place for Hob and Jack and Macha between them.

"Jack! When are you going to marry that little dog?" This, with much thumping of Jack's arms and ruffling of Sweetlove's head, brought forth a grin and a nod from Jack, and from Sweetlove, that one-man loyalist, a discreet grumble, a tiny lifting of the lip to show just the gleaming tips of sharp white teeth.

"Now he's finally married Lucinda," said Ranulf, "he's preaching marriage to every man and maid—ha! and now every man and dog!"

"Why, my congratulations," said Hob, shaking his hand. "I wish you joy of your union, Roger." Jack, avoiding speech, just slapped him on the back.

For such a hardened soldier, with his face sun-darkened, scars here and there, Roger suddenly looked quite shy. "She's with child, Lucinda. 'Twill be by Michaelmas."

Now there was another round of congratulations. "And have you a name for the bairn?" asked Hob.

"If it's a girl, we'll name it 'Avis,' after Lucinda's grandmother," said Roger. "It will be 'Olivier' if it's a boy."

"Ah," said Hob. "That's well done, then." Olivier was Roger's great friend, killed on Fox Night back in Castle Blanchefontaine.

Away across the stretch of grass, over by the stables, Nemain was leading out the two mares, already hitched to the war chariot. Roger leaned out from the wall in order to address Hob past Jack's body.

"Sir Robert, tell us something: there's talk of a dangerous wight, Robert the Englishman, a commoner, one who slew a mort of pirates on the crossing from Chester to Dublin, and some are saying that it was you slew them, and others are saying that Sir Robert and Robert the Englishman are not the same man, and I've a bet that 'twas you, for there was talk of two women with bows and a big lad with a hammer, and who else could that be?"

"Well," began Hob, but then Jack held up an outstretched palm—*Wait!*—and then indicated Hob with his thumb. Hob just grinned and nodded. Roger stretched an open hand across toward Ranulf, and the sergeant dropped a small coin into it.

Across the bailey Nemain jumped into the chariot and took up the reins; Molly stepped in beside her, one hand to the rail and the other with four javelins that she placed in one of the car-side cylinders. The younger woman flicked the reins and the horses walked forward; the small car began to roll, the two high wheels making for an easy passage over the uneven ground. A whistle, and the horses picked up pace, breaking into a trot.

Two quintains had been set up, one thirty feet behind the other. The first was a post with a fixed arm from which depended a string; the string ended in an iron ring, perhaps an inch and a half in diameter. The second had a movable arm with a target painted in concentric circles, connected to a second arm with a sandbag attached. The object of the exercise at the first quintain was to put a javelin through the ring; at the second quintain the task was to hit the target with a lance—which would bring the sandbag flying around the pole to strike the lancer—while going quickly enough to escape being hit.

Nemain took them around the perimeter of the bailey to warm them up, then stopped at the far side. A piercing cry from her and the horses sprang into a gallop, racing in a wide circle. Nemain then executed a series of breathtaking changes of direction, finally pulling the horses around at the lower end of the grassy field, and charging straight at the first quintain.

Molly drew a javelin up from a chariot-side scabbard, tossed and caught it so that she had it in an overhand grip, and drew back her strong white arm for a cast. The chariot thundered down the middle of the bailey. The whole car bounced and left the ground when it hit irregularities or buried stones in the field, the women easily keeping their balance, one hand to the wicker rail, knees flexing with each upward bound, each downward jolt. Through all this chaos

Molly kept her javelin steady and as they drew near the first quintain, she cast it, the slim spearhead threading the eye of the iron ring, the shaft carrying on through the circlet till its increasing width caused it to stick fast. The javelin hung suspended from the arm of the quintain, halfway through the ring.

Without slacking speed, they hurtled on toward the second quintain. Molly drew up another javelin from the scabbard, reversed grip, and as they reached the target stabbed it dead center, sending the arm on its swivel greased with lard flying away from them, the sandbag at the end of its rope tilting outward with centrifugal force, whirling past them just too late as Nemain ran the mares full tilt down the bailey. The weighted canvas bag shot by past the women's backs, slapping just the tips of the blood-red mane, the silver mane, that were streaming out behind them.

A page ran out and tugged both javelins free, set the target in the proper position, stilled the spinning ring. Nemain was coming around in a wide semicircle, and then she was in position downfield, and made another run at the target. Again Molly pierced the ring, and they barreled on toward the second quintain, and this time Molly threw at the target instead of stabbing it and there was a flickering silver wheel beside her javelin as it flew at the quintain. Again they avoided the sandbag, and in addition to the javelin fast in the wood at the edge of the inner circle, there was Nemain's dagger stuck quivering in the dead center of the target.

The men at the side wall were all on their feet cheering by this time, Macha shouting war cries in Irish, her clear high child's voice echoing from the bailey walls. Sweetlove was barking in support of their enthusiasm, uncertain though she was about its subject. Nemain slowed the horses to a walk, then set out on a slow perambulation about the sward, to give the animals a chance to cool down.

"Fuck!" said Roger. "I'd bet that they'd miss at least once." He handed the coin back to Ranulf.

"I'd not want to see them charging toward me," said Ranulf, fumbling with his pouch strings, dropping the coin in. "If that throw-spear didna spit you, the dagger'd end up in your eye." He nodded to Hob. "A dangerous woman, your lady wife, Sir Robert!"

"She never fails to surprise me," said Hob in all honesty. He looked out on the field. Nemain was driving the chariot past Molly at a good clip, and the older woman was practicing grabbing at the hand rail and jumping upward, letting the chariot's velocity snatch her aboard. "They're one more surprising than the other."

Chapter 14

They were most of the way there, and the senior knights beginning to speak of the value of surprise, when the ambush came.

There had been a rapid progress up the coast road, with barren land to their right and the great Western Ocean stretching away to the edge of the world on their left, in their ears the roar-and-sigh, roar-and-sigh of the waves, waves such as Hob had never seen, battering at the borders of the land. Molly had told him once, as he stood there entranced at his first sight of the German Sea stretching eastward from the northeast coast of England, that when he saw the Western Ocean he would think this a puddle. He had not been disappointed; if anything, the great waters exceeded his imagination. He found rivers, lakes, oceans entrancing: anywhere there was a large amount of water, preferably with movement, either the onward unreturning rush of stream and river or the huge repetitive breathing movements of sea and ocean, and the Western Ocean was a joy to him whenever he contemplated it.

The order of march had some mounted Irish kerns first, deployed as scouts, followed by the vanguard of Norman knights, led by Sir Balthasar, with Hob as his second-in-command. Then came Molly's war chariot, with Nemain driving, and Jack marching right behind; baggage and supply wagons came next, secure in the middle of the column, with Irish footsoldiers riding atop the loads or walking beside. Following the last wain were the company of Welsh archers, their great longbows strung and slung over their shoulders, ready at a moment's notice, and then the remaining two Norman groups: the battle, commanded by Sir Jehan, who was overall warleader under Molly, and the rearguard, commanded by Sir Odinell.

They crossed streams at fords and rivers at bridges, always moving northward. The sun was sailing up toward noon, and they had begun just before daybreak. Sir Jehan had them halt by a cold little stream for a meal of hard cheese and rich dark bread. The animals were watered, and then they moved on, for the Ó Cearbhaill homelands were just up the coast.

Across their path was a set of three small mountains, marking the southern border of Ó Cearbhaill land. The Christians to the south of Molly's lands called them The Trinity; Molly's tribe called them The Mórrígan. The westernmost mountain stood with its feet in the sea. Between that mountain and the middle one—the Son to the Christians, Babd to the pagans—the road rose to a pass. Once through that pass, the column would be visible from the valley beyond, where Sir Jehan hoped to descend and spread his battle line across the southern high slopes.

It was a well-kept hard-packed dirt road, with hedges along both sides. As they began to toil upward on a slight grade, the hedges began to increase in height. Hob found himself growing uneasy; the hedges were almost to his shoulders, mounted though he was on tall Iarann. He peered at them: they seemed unnaturally dense, with thorns as long as his thumb, and the sunlight struggled to seep through the tight-packed stems and leaves.

He heard a disturbance behind him, and Nemain calling his name. He reined in and looked around. Here came Nemain trotting up the line toward the head of Sir Balthasar's vanguard. Sir Balthasar gave the signal to halt, and the column of knights behind them pulled up. Nemain reached up a hand to Hob's knee, and addressed Sir Balthasar.

"Sure there's an ambush of some kind laid for us here," she said, panting a bit. "These hedges—they're plashed, and we're in a channel. Sir Jehan says we should halt and get some axmen to cut a gateway."

Hob looked again at the hedges. They had indeed been plashed: of each four thick plant stems, three were cut halfway through near the ground and then bent sideways, and the fourth left upright, augmented by upright stakes. The sideways stems were woven through the uprights, and then they sent up shoots from their upper sides, and the result was a woven hedge, armed with thorns, that was impenetrably thick. No one could push his way through, and even cutting was long laborious work. Essentially the road now ran between living walls.

The way just ahead curved around a bend, and while they had been talking the mounted Irish scouts had gone around and out of sight. Now they came spurring back and drew up sharply, the Irish ponies' hooves kicking up clods of dirt. A veil of dust around their legs drifted into the base of the hedge.

The chief scout, a man named Fergus, said, stuttering a bit in excitement, "There's a ditch and a rampart, and on it isn't there a squad of monstrous gallowglasses with their mail and axes, and they barring the way."

Nemain looked back along the column, but there was no time to run and consult with Molly or Sir Jehan. She held up a hand; she was thinking of everything Molly had told her of Irish tactics, and she said, "These will be watchmen; they'll hold us here while they send some messenger back, and the whole of the Uí Bháis will be waiting for us at the top of the pass. We've no time to return now, nor to chop through this hedge. We must go through them."

Gallowglasses, as Molly had said, always had two squires who attended each of them, and armed them, and carried their baggage. In battle, though, the squires acted as light skirmishers; they wore no armor, and ran swiftly toward the enemy, and threw light javelins that they carried, three to a squire. Now javelins began to rain into the lane;

Hob wheeled Iarann around, seeking the source. He noticed movement in the trees beyond the hedges.

"They are in the trees!" he shouted.

"Shields!" bellowed Sir Balthasar.

Hob pulled his shield from its saddle mount and held it over Nemain's head. "You!" he called to one of the scouts, his mount fidgeting in the lane, holding his round targe over his head. "Take Queen Nemain back to her chariot."

She sprang up behind the scout and Hob handed her the shield.

"Nay," she said, and, cool-tempered as she always was in danger, was unable to resist her little jest even as death whistled and thudded in around them: "Even your thick skull cannot withstand a javelin."

"Go, you little brat," he said, something from their childhood together. He thrust the shield into her arms and slapped the scout's mount and they went on back down the line.

Sir Balthasar had been growling orders left and right. "You men, back down to that long wagon and knock a plank off each sideboard and run them up here. You there, go back to the Welshmen and have them up on the wagon loads. Tell them to rake the trees. Fergus, tell Sir Jehan what is occurring here. Sir Robert, let's around that bend and see what's toward."

They trotted their horses up and around the curve. There was another thirty-yard stretch and then the road was cut from hedge to hedge with a deep trench, perhaps six feet wide. From this angle they could not be sure of the depth, but it looked deeper than it was wide. On the far side of the ditch a berm had been thrown up, using the soil from the trench. Atop the barrier was a waist-high parapet of wooden mantlets, large rectangular shields staked into the soil of the berm.

Behind this was a line of eight huge Norse Gaels, clad in their long mail hauberks, their padded gloves with knuckle plates, their helmets with cheekpieces that curved around, leaving a slit in front as wide as a man's thumb was long. Into this slit depended the nasal, filling the top two-thirds; the result was a mask that showed the eyes, a portion of the mouth. From the eyeholes pale eyes looked forth, expressionless. The gallowglasses' stance suggested immovability. On their shoulders rested the heads of their long sparth axes, terrible crescent-bladed two-handed weapons.

Sir Balthasar spat. "Well, let us go through them." He sent messengers back to the knights of the vanguard, instructing them to dismount and advance on foot. "Sir Robert, you and I will go up first: 'tis only courtesy to knock politely at their door."

Men-at-arms were trotting up with ten-foot planks, torn from the sides of the wagons. Sir Balthasar told off men with shields to cover the men carrying the boards, and sent them at the ditch. They ran up, dropped the two planks across the gap, and retreated, shields held high. Hob moved the reins against Iarann's neck, lining him up with the board. The planks would never support the weight of a destrier, but the two knights would sweep up to the boards and then dismount.

Around the bend behind them came the Norman knights of the vanguard, dismounted, running with their horseman's axes in hand, bearing the smaller half-shields on their left arms.

Two javelins came hissing in; one hit Hob a glancing blow on his shoulder blade, the small lancehead skittering off his mail. The other swept an Irish scout from his horse, the flexible shaft embedded in his chest. He fell with a clatter in the road, dropping his own lance; he moved just a bit, and then again, and then died.

Sir Balthasar looked at Hob. The castellan unshipped his horseman's ax from his saddle, and Hob did the same. Then: "Blanchefontaine!" roared the castellan in a voice one might use to frighten a lion, and spurred his destrier straight at the trench. "*Banríon Maeve abú!*" shouted Hob, and kneed Iarann into a run.

A few yards shy of the gap, Sir Balthasar pulled up short, his horse with front hooves braced stiff-legged and spraying a fan of dirt into the trench beyond. He threw himself out of the saddle and Hob pulled up beside him.

One of the gallowglasses had hooked a plank with his ax and tipped it into the trench, leaving only one path across. Sir Balthasar sprang onto this plank and trotted across, the plank flexing and bowing beneath him. With fifty pounds of iron on his body, he was about three hundredweight, and he was not a corpulent man. Hob dismounted and ran onto the plank after Sir Balthasar, hoping it would not fail beneath their combined burden.

But the castellan was off the wood and onto the far bank

in a moment, and Hob himself was right on Sir Balthasar's heels. The castellan reached the line of mantlets first; a tremendous kick from his armored shoe against the mantlet's side twisted the big ground-shield on its spike, creating an opening and putting one gallowglass off balance. Two more of the Norse Gaels aimed their long bearded axes at Sir Balthasar, and Hob, struggling up the bank, saw the Norman perform an astonishing feat: with the upper edge of his shield he smote upward against one opponent's wrists—the downward force of the Hebridean's blow broke the small bones in his own forearms, the long ax flying free and embedding itself in the bermside dirt. Simultaneously Sir Balthasar blocked the other gallowglass axhead with the spiked ax he carried in his right hand, managing to tangle the beard of his foe's long ax with his spike. He pulled, hauling the gallowglass forward; the man tumbled down the short berm to lie before Hob, who drove the spike of his own ax into the man's skull.

Then Sir Balthasar was through the line, on a level with the other gallowglasses, and turning to attack them. A moment later Hob rushed through the gap and narrowly evaded a whickering ax blade rushing past his face. He parried the next blow, barely catching the stroke on the top edge of his own ax. The blow numbed his arm, but his attacker was left off-balance. Hob reversed his ax and hammered with the spike at the man's chest. The spike went partway through the mail and snagged in the padded gambeson beneath, but the force of the blow staggered the Hebridean backward, and seemed to deprive him of all breath. Hob hacked at his leg below the hauberk with the blade of his ax, and felt something sever: the man went down, wheezing and seeking to spin and fight upward. A dagger had materialized in his left hand, but Hob was too fast and too strong—he stamped on the gallowglass's left forearm, swiveled his ax in his hand, and planted the spike in the helmet's narrow ocular opening, beside the nasal. The gallowglass convulsed, and then was dead.

The knights of the vanguard were pouring through the gap Sir Balthasar and Hob had opened. The first two knights did not fare well: the long-shafted gallowglass axes fell like thunderbolts upon them, splitting a shield here and cleaving through a mailed shoulder there; one Norman was nearly beheaded by a tremendous blow from one of the huge Norse Gaels. But then the gallowglasses were going down, each swarmed by two or three Normans.

Sir Balthasar had lost his own weapon, but was holding the shaft of a gallowglass's ax just above the Hebridean's hands; with one hand he resisted the foeman's two-armed effort to bring the ax down. Even as Hob moved to help him, he saw the castellan draw back his right fist, encased in a gauntlet that had a row of blunt spikes along the knuckles, and punch into the man's ribs. There was a shriek—Hob thought immediately of a broken rib—and the man tried to pull away from Sir Balthasar. The Norman now managed to draw his dagger and stab upward under the gallowglass's chin, killing him.

Hob saw that the castellan was out of danger, and turned to one of the remaining Hebrideans. The man shuffled sideways, positioning himself for a circular blow, the heavy gauntlets clutching the long haft in a woodcutter's grip. Hob threw his ax at the man's face, and the gallowglass, with professional ease, almost contemptuously slipped the blow, moving his head just enough so that the ax skidded off the side of the helmet.

But Hob had used the momentary distraction to come inside the reach of the sparth, diving forward with his war dagger in his hand, driven with all the force of his big body behind it. He was no Sir Balthasar, but he was nearly two hundredweight naked and with the weight of his mail adding another fifty or so pounds, the sharp point and thick-backed blade of the dagger split links in the Hebridean's mail, punched through the padding beneath, slanting up under the man's breastbone, bursting his heart.

The gallowglass crashed over backward, and Hob swung about, ready for another enemy who never appeared. The eight men of the Uí Bháis were dead, as were two of Castle Blanchefontaine's knights. Sir Balthasar looked about him. He stamped back across the makeshift bridge; there the Irish scouts were clustered on their small swift horses.

"Fergus, send one of your men back to the men-at-arms; tell Sergeant Ranulf to get some shovels from the wains, and tell off a detail to come up here and fill in this fucking ditch. You—tell the quartermaster we need two canvas winding sheets—I've got two of my own slain here; send up that chaplain, that Irish priest, what's his—Father Brendan. Ah, God and Mary with you, mesdames; greeting, brother."

This last was to Molly and Nemain, and Sir Jehan, who had come forward to see what transpired. Nemain, after a burning glance around the company till she located Hob, obviously unharmed, on the far side of the trench, returned her attention to the castellan.

"The way is clear, once we fill in the gap and tamp it down a bit," growled Sir Balthasar.

Molly said, "One does not plash hedges overnight—it takes years. So this is a barrier that is always here, and these are to delay while a warning is sent to the valley beyond. We must make all haste from here on."

"We must fill—" began the castellan again.

"Nay, they cannot have filled it in every time a welcome party sought to use the pass," said Molly. She and Nemain went and closely inspected the hedges just before the trench, each taking a different side. Sir Jehan and Sir Balthasar watched, bemused, as the women walked back and forth, at one point getting down on all fours.

"Here 'tis, *seanmháthair*," called Nemain.

Hidden behind the leaves were two posts joined by hidden latches. Nemain released the latches and pushed, walking forward; a whole section of hedge was planted in a box that moved on wooden wheels. The box itself was camouflaged with nailed-on branches; in the heat of an ambush no one would think to look closely at this particular segment of the green wall.

"Precious Christ!" said Sir Balthasar. A section of the hedge wide as a large barn door was now open, and a semicircular path behind it led around the end of the trench to rejoin the road behind the berm. From that point on the road was open on either hand.

"Get them moving, brother," said Sir Jehan. "Certes, the alarm has sped north toward our foes." He and Molly began to walk back to their places in the column. Nemain blew Hob a kiss and turned to follow her grandmother.

Sir Balthasar bellowed orders. The knights of the vanguard went back to remount their destriers. The scouts poured through the gap and began to fan out toward the north, once more testing the land. Hob swung up onto Iarann, and Sir Balthasar vaulted into his own saddle. He turned and signaled the advance, and walked his horse through the gap. Hob fell in beside him, as the castellan drew a cloth from his saddle pouch and began to wipe gore and bits of flesh from the spiked knuckles of his gauntlets.

Hob looked back along the outside of the hedge. Beneath the trees, here and there, like a ghastly windfall, were the bodies of the gallowglass squires, feathered with arrows: the long Welsh clothyard arrows and the black-fletched crow-feather arrows favored by Molly and Nemain.

When they had regained the proper road, Sir Balthasar picked up the pace, for as he said, " 'Twill be a close-run race to see who can reach the field of battle first, and who can first dispose themselves for battle."

Chapter 15

Up the steepening slope they toiled, to where the road ran through a slot between the mountains, the vast bulk of stone slanting up to either hand, ending in peaks far above. They moved through shadow, the mountains on each side blocking the light. Hob, concentrating on guiding Iarann's steps on the rock-strewn upper reaches of the pass, suddenly became aware of increased light. He looked up; they were nearly at the top of the pass, and the sunlight came in level here. The notch brightened further, and then they were through, and the valley of the Ó Cearbhaills spread out before them.

The valley slanted down toward the west, down to where the Western Ocean broke on stony beaches. To the north there were mountains, and the northern shoreline rose to high sheer cliffs. Where the land rose toward the northern foothills was the stronghold of the Ó Cearbhaills, now occupied by the brutal Uí Bháis.

The column descended halfway to the valley floor, and then Sir Balthasar led his vanguard to the right, to take up the right flank. He arranged the men-at-arms in a loose rectangular formation; behind them lurked the mailed knights. When he had them disposed to his satisfaction, he said to Hob, "Let us find Sir Jehan and Queen Maeve and see what is toward."

They made their way behind the groups of archers, men-at-arms, Irish kerns, squires, and knights rapidly sorting themselves into battle order. Behind all, up the slope where they could oversee the entire field of conflict, Molly and Nemain stood beside their war chariot with Sir Jehan, Sir Odinell, and three Irishmen: Bróccan, Daire, and a man Hob did not recognize. The two knights rode up and dismounted.

"Ah, here you are, brother," said Sir Jehan. He had exchanged his bronze hand for a steel hand that he wore on campaign; it bore the same legend as the bronze, but in silver. This steel glove was fastened to his arm by a cunning bracelet as well as straps that ran up to his elbow. The hand could be clamped upon the bracket of a shield, and Sir Jehan had learned to fight all over again, training with his left hand holding the sword, hence the legend, *Cave Sinistram.*

Molly indicated the third Irishman and said to the newcomers, "This is my cousin Cabhan; he has a small farm up the hill, and has been forced to live under these Norse-Gael murderers, and to pay them tribute. He knows much of their doings, and has been waiting and hoping for our return." Hob saw a man of about fifty summers, lean, balding, bitter-eyed. He wore the usual Irish costume of a *léine*, a cloak, a broad belt with pouch and dagger. He was barefoot and barelegged; he leaned on a thick blackthorn staff.

Suddenly Molly pointed across the valley. "There they are, the spalpeens, defiling my home as they are."

Hob turned to look. The fortress of the Ó Cearbhaills was a modified rath, a ring fort built up from an earlier enclosed farming village. Set on a hill, Molly's stronghold was surrounded by a berm of earth surmounted by wooden palisade walls; outside the walls was a deep ditch. Within the walls was a cluster of buildings, some wood, some wattle-and-daub, with a wooden tower in the center. Through the tall main gates marched three battles of gallowglasses, quickly deploying in a line across the front of the fortress. All wore hauberks, mail shirts that reached from throat to knee, over quilted gambesons, and conical helmets that covered much of their faces; all bore two-handed axes. The effect was one of grim implacability, of more-than-human or less-than-human foes.

Behind them came their squires, two to each gallowglass, apprentice gallowglasses who served as auxiliaries and skirmishers for their heavily armed masters. These squires trotted through the aisles between the gallowglass battles to take up position in front of the line of mailed men. And now to either side came the rabble of outlaws, mercenaries, and masterless men that the Uí Bháis had attracted, using them to augment the limited manpower of the tribe, and employing them as enforcers against those of Molly's people who, unable to escape as had Daire and Bróccan, had been trapped and pressed into servitude, farming the land for Queen Ferelith and her warrior tribesmen.

And last came Herself, *Banríon* Ferelith, in a two-horse chariot driven by a man in a tunic and cloak, but without armor.

"There she is!" cried Cabhan. "The evil witch! She has borne three sons, and the gods took each one, punishment for her wickedness. She has worked us and taxed us and killed any who shirked. You will kill her, will you not, my queen, my cousin? For our people, for what they have suffered!" His face was reddening; a vessel pulsed in his temple.

Molly was watching the other woman, away there on the far side of the little valley. She spoke without taking her eyes from Ferelith. She raised her white hand as if to display it to Cabhan, and said, "I will kill her, cousin; by She Whom I swear by, I will kill her with this hand."

And as if she could hear Molly, down there the usurper queen raised her head and looked up at the slope where the Normans had formed their usual tripartite battle formation, where the Welsh archers were wrestling fresh strings onto their six-foot bows, where the returned exiles of Molly's tribe were gathering on the wings to right and left of the Norman knights and men-at-arms. She looked up past all these preparations for war, and directly at the knoll where Molly's chariot was halted. She was so far away that Hob could not actually tell the focus of her eyes, but the tilt of her head left no doubt that she was looking at the little group of commanders.

Then she did an extraordinary thing: she took a targe from its hook on the side of the chariot, and put her right arm through the braces; then she spoke to her charioteer, and the man whipped up his horses, and the chariot went along behind her gallowglasses and around their right flank, and headed across the valley floor and up the slope toward the waiting army. She was on the right side of her chariot, and her driver stood on the left, so that when they reached the Norman left flank and turned along the front of the invaders, she was nearer to Molly's army, with only the small round shield to protect her.

They drove all along the front of the drawn-up host, at a deliberate pace, and she stood tall and erect, and glared over the heads of the knights at Molly up on her knoll. Hob saw a tall woman with wide-set piercing dark eyes, a nose that was not overlong, but straight and quite thick, a determined chin, all of it giving an impression of great strength of will. Her entire stance spoke of arrogance. She might be reviewing her own troops, thought Hob.

"Precious Christ! She does not lack for courage," said Sir Balthasar, with a tinge of admiration creeping into his growling bass.

Llewellyn ap Dafydd, the commander of the Welsh archers, appeared at Molly's side. He was a man a bit above middle height, with the burly shoulders of the professional archer: it was said that his bow had a draw somewhere between one and two hundredweight. He looked from Molly to Sir Jehan, his blue eyes, round, prominent, heavy-lidded, trying to decide the correct person to address first.

"My lord, my lady, I'm thinking, see you, God with me, I could put an arrow into yon witch, and there's our end to battle, isn't there?" He was speaking English, but with so strong a lilt that he might have been singing.

" 'Tis unchivalrous," growled Sir Balthasar unexpectedly.

"But effective," said Sir Jehan, who tended to the sardonic rather than the sentimental.

"I thank you, friend Llewellyn," said Molly, "but, not to put too fine a point on it, she is my meat and mine alone, and I mean to kill her and I mean to wash my hands in her blood."

This was said with such quiet ferocity that Sir Odinell looked at her with some dismay, but Sir Balthasar just nodded grimly.

Queen Ferelith had reached the far end of the Norman line and now turned back down the valley. She reached the gallowglass line, which opened to receive her, and her charioteer brought her to the rear of her army, turned the two-wheeled car so that it faced forward, and set the brake. The two armies now stood quietly while final small adjustments were made on each side: a squad moved more to the west, or javelin throwers moved farther out from the main force, and the like.

The sun moved down the sky; the breeze ruffled the wildflowers dotted here and there in the grass; small birds landed at random, hopped about, pecked at things unseen, heedless of the maneuvers of men.

AT LAST QUEEN FERELITH spoke a word to the runners poised by her chariot. Two ran in opposite directions and gave instructions to the crowds of Irish mercenaries crouched on either wing of her army. These fought in the Irish style, with no armor, clad only in shirts and cloaks, running lightly forward, barefoot on the sloping grass. They ran to within yards of the Norman lines and cast light javelins. A rain of these spears fell amid the Normans, but did only sporadic damage—the shields of the knights and men-at-arms, and the mail of the knights, stopped or turned most of the missiles. Here and there a man went down, and then the mercenaries drew forth the second javelins that had been slung to their backs.

But Molly had loosed her tribesmen, those who had returned from their forced exile, and they closed from either side upon the mercenaries: savage fighting, javelin against javelin, the light short spears held midway and stabbed overhand at the enemy. The Irish style emphasized speed and ferocity: men leaped to the attack, leaped back, hacking at one another with short one-hand axes and straight swords with ring pommels, without armor and with only small round shields.

All were experienced warriors, but the Uí Bháis mercenaries had been recruited from among outlaws and other men of brutal temperament and little virtue; on the other side were Molly's returned clan exiles, fighting to regain their homeland and to free their kinsmen enslaved by the Hebrideans and forced to work the land for them. The difference in spirit soon told, and the mercenaries broke and ran, pursued toward the gallowglass ranks by howling Ó Cearbhaill tribesmen.

Every gallowglass was attended by two squires, who

hoped to advance to gallowglass rank eventually. As the mercenaries neared the gallowglass ranks, these squires ran out from behind the mailed axmen and cast javelins at Molly's clansmen. Many of the mercenaries kept on going, running off to the east and the shelter of the bordering forest; some ran behind the ranks of the gallowglass and re-formed, awaiting orders. Some of Molly's warriors had shields, but most did not, and the rain of javelins thrown by very well-trained men, chosen for their size and strength as all gallowglasses were, served to break their pursuit of the fleeing mercenaries. Molly's men went down all along their battle front, and a retreat was sounded, hale men dragging the wounded from the field, while still the squires' spears hissed down all around them.

The squires each had three javelins, and they threw the first two and attacked with the third. Now the mass of squires began to pursue the retreating tribesmen, hoping to kill as many from behind as possible. Those of Molly's people who were mounted, generally from the wealthier families that had a horse, had been kept off to the left flank; now they rode at the squires, whipping past and killing on the run and swooping away to the right flank. These were light hit-and-run cavalry, without saddles or stirrups, and could not deliver the heavy blow of a mailed cavalry charge; in some ways well-planted footsoldiers could with not too much difficulty ground the butts of their spears or pikes and unhorse the Irish cavalry, unbraced as they were without cantle or stirrup.

They had slowed the squires' pursuit of the Irish clansmen on foot; now Molly had them recalled, and Sir Jehan turned to the Welsh captain. "Llewellyn, clear away those gallowglass squires."

Cupping his hands over his mouth, ap Dafydd bellowed orders in Welsh. The heavy-shouldered archers came running up the open aisles between the three groups of Norman knights, spread out into squads of ten, who fitted an arrow to the string, drew back to their ears, and loosed their shafts, all to a rhythmic chant from their sergeants. The squires were half the way toward the Norman line, and the flights of arrows, arriving in unison, knocked immediate gaps in their lines. They faltered, and then a trumpet called from the far end of the field, and they fell back, the clothyard arrows continuing to hum among them, men falling steadily, the ranks thinning and thinning, till they reached the gallowglass line and took refuge behind the mailed wall.

The archers had gone to individual shooting, and they had trotted after the squires, pausing to loose a shaft and advancing another ten feet or so, till they had reached the midway line between the two hosts, and now, like one of the waves crashing against the rocks below, the gallowglass line surged forward with a deep shout and charged toward Molly's host.

Hob thought that such large men, so heavily mailed and with such large axes, would advance at a stately pace, but the gallowglasses went from a fast walk to a trot in moments, and while they ran they bellowed war cries, overlapping so that all one could make out was a deep continuous roar.

Ap Dafydd called the retreat on a horn slung about his

chest, and the archers turned and ran for the Norman lines. There was no chance of them fighting hand to hand with these armored giants.

Sir Jehan tried a difficult maneuver: he had his men-at-arms, many of them with pikes, run out to the sides and curve back in, so that instead of opposing the gallowglass charge directly, they came in at a slant and attacked the left and right wings. The men-at-arms of Castles Blanchefontaine and Chantemerle, hardy soldiers in boiled-leather gambesons, were able to harry the gallowglasses and slow the charge on the right and on the left, but where gallowglass groups turned on them and engaged them directly, the difference in size and armor told: the long axes rose and fell, hacking through the gambesons, while a sword or dagger thrust often was turned aside by the heavy mail hauberks.

Three gallowglasses, fighting turned slightly away from each other, made an entity that defended itself on three sides, and the long reach of the axes made it difficult even to land a blow. Hob found himself wondering how Ranulf and Roger and other friends of his from the castles were faring. But the footsoldiers' attacks on the gallowglass wings had shredded away a certain number of the Hebridean axmen, and slacked the momentum of their advance, and now Sir Jehan ordered his trumpeter to sound the charge. Hob had already taken his place by Sir Balthasar, and now he settled his helm and took a lance from one of the squires.

Iarann was tense beneath him; the destriers always

seemed to know, perhaps from a sense of their riders' posture, the clasp of their legs, when the command to go was about to be given. When the golden notes rang out over the field, he touched the spurs to the big gray horse's flanks, and they moved out at a walk, the three battles—Sir Odinell's on the left flank, Sir Jehan's in the middle, and Sir Balthasar's on the right where Hob was stationed—moving out in an even line.

The gallowglasses, seeing what was about to happen, halted where they were, a little past the halfway mark, and tightened their line. Another call from Sir Jehan's trumpeter, and the group moved to a trot, and soon they were at full gallop, an earthslide of massive horses and mailed men, the drumming of the hooves blurring into a continuous roll of thunder, the lances with their fluttering pennants at the tips coming down, couched with a jolt against the knights' sides, a many-horned beast bearing down on the gallowglass wall.

The knights crashed into the Hebridean formation, lances punching a hole right through the mail, knights dropping the lance after the first impact and drawing sword or mace and striking, striking downward, like reapers working their way into a field.

Hob felt the jar of his lance into the front-line gallowglass he had aimed for, and rode Iarann into the press of Hebridean warriors. The lance, embedded in his victim, was dragged from his glove as the destrier plowed forward. He pulled the horseman's ax from its saddle sheath, secured his grip, and swung downward at any gallowglass who came within his reach. Axes reached for him, and he banged them away with his shield. He struck at a looming gallowglass, hacking at an angle to get the little unprotected area between helmet and hauberk; the blow jarred his arm to the shoulder, but he had nearly beheaded the man.

Many in the first line of the gallowglasses had gone down, speared or simply trampled under the great hooves, but the tight-packed gallowglass formation soon slowed the knights' forward momentum, and now came the turn of the Hebrideans, who used the beard of their ax blade to hook a knight under the belt or by the baldric and haul him straight out of the saddle. The fastest, most agile knights might roll to their feet and engage their attackers, but several, slammed against the earth and stunned for a moment, were hacked to death moments later as two or three gallowglasses swung their great axes down upon the fallen foe.

Beneath him, Iarann struck forward with his hooves; in addition to the deadly force of his kick, the fronts of his horseshoes were augmented with projecting spikes. The horse was also snapping at the faces of the Norse Gael axmen, and as he went for a gallowglass, veering leftward, he inadvertently saved Hob's leg, for an axhead whistled past his knee. The man had struck from slightly behind Hob, and as he attempted to recover, a huge shadow loomed over him: Sir Balthasar on his destrier, striking down with the bottom of his shield, the powerful knight breaking the gallowglass's neck.

"Sir Balthasar!" Hob shouted, by way of acknowledgment.

The Blanchefontaine castellan raised his sword in salute. "Giant's-bane!" Then it was back to killing.

They were in a real melee now. The noise was deafening: the shouting of men—war cries, cries of dismay—and the clang of weapons, the neighing and occasional screams of horses, the laments of the wounded, and the thud of hooves on the earth and the grinding of mail against mail as the gallowglasses fought shoulder to shoulder. There was a crash near Hob as a knight was pulled from his saddle. He looked down; Sir Odinell was on the ground and Sir Balthasar now leaped from his saddle to stand over his fallen friend. A knot of five gallowglasses surrounded both men; Sir Odinell, stunned, struggled to regain his feet.

Hob swung down from his horse and clove his way through the three or four feet separating him from the two knights. He reached Sir Balthasar and stood back-to-back with the castellan. Axheads flew at them from every direction. The blows from the huge men were numbing Hob's shield arm, while he hacked like a madman at a succession of apparitions in knitted steel. The mail was dulled with the dust hurled into the air from hoof and heel. He dodged, feinted, hampered by the necessity to remain in one place to guard Sir Balthasar's back. His arm rose and fell; he killed one man, then another; he fended off a blow from a tall axman and struck at the man's arm, but the angle was poor and the blade skidded off the mail. A moment later one of the Chantemerle knights pounded past and put a lance into Hob's opponent, killing him. The space in front of Hob was, at least for the moment, clear of enemies.

Even through the din of battle, Hob could hear the blows rained upon the Hebrideans by Sir Balthasar. As formidable as were the Norse Gaels, the Blanchefontaine castellan was more like a tiger than a man: massive, with a wild-beast ferocity and a strength second only to Jack's and an extensive knowledge of weaponry and its use. And now Sir Odinell, a staunch if uninspired fighter, was back on his feet. Hob became aware of a slackening of pressure from the axmen around. He buried the spike portion of his horseman's ax in an opponent's chest, piercing mail and the padded gambeson below, a mortal wound; Hob had to bash his shield against the gallowglass's shoulder, pushing him back, before he could free the spike.

He looked around: the gallowglasses were retreating in a tight formation; the knights of castles Blanchefontaine and Chantemerle were riding around the periphery, picking off a man here and there. The battle was receding from the three dismounted knights, and as Hob watched, axes flicked out from the knot of Hebrideans and killed a horse under one of the knights. Hob could not tell who it was from here, though he knew them all. Whoever it was had the misfortune to fall from his collapsing mount in the direction of the gallowglass phalanx, and he was immediately hewed to death.

Iarann was waiting for him nearby, as he had been

trained to do, and Hob mounted, but the gallowglasses had reached their walls, and the protection of their archers and javelineers, and Sir Jehan had the retreat-and-regroup sounded.

The knights repaired to their original position on the hill where Molly waited, overlooking the field.

Chapter 16

THE SENIOR KNIGHTS GATHERED NEAR the chariot. The gallowglass numbers were much reduced, and Sir Balthasar urged a full bathe-in-their-blood attack, with everyone charging down the hill. Sir Odinell, more cautious, thought they should advance halfway and employ the Welsh to thin the gallowglass ranks even more before the final charge.

But Molly was looking away down the hill to where the other queen was speaking with a tall older man, swathed in an oak-brown cloak, with a harp case slung to his back. "Pause a moment, my brave champions. There's something afoot over there, and I'm thinking we're about to hear an offer."

The harper strode through the gallowglass lines and up the hill toward Molly's position. She said to Sir Jehan, "Tell your men under no circumstance to harm that man; he's a bard, and in Erin they are sacred." Sir Jehan passed the order down to the Normans; the Welsh and the Irish already knew to hold their hands.

Up the bard toiled with long vigorous strides, his cloak billowing behind him in the constant breezes from the Western Ocean, so close at hand. Fine boots of brown cordwain rose to his knee; red-brown hose covered his legs; his hands had gold rings on almost every finger, the usual reward for a performance from princes. He halted twenty paces short of the Norman lines, a man in early middle years, with long unruly brown hair, a thick streak of silver at each temple. He called out in a rich deep baritone, "Hear me! I am Turlough of Armagh, and I bring an offer of trial by combat, from Ferelith queen of the Uí Bháis to Maeve queen of the Ó Cearbhaills: the loser to surrender all claim to this land, and to leave this place forever."

At this Sir Odinell, bold as a bear in combat but distrusting of unconventional arrangements, began to protest.

"Surely it is better not to risk all on one throw of the die, Madam," he began. "And there may be an ambush, some treachery that that bard—"

"Nay, Sir Odinell, I had expected that it might come to single combat between Ferelith and myself, and in fact I had hoped for it, and had she not challenged me I would have challenged her."

Hob and Jack had heard this discussed many times, on quiet nights in the big wagon, and so they were not surprised, but to the Normans a duel between two women, with the outcome deciding the battle, was unheard of. Sir Jehan, cool of temperament, showed nothing but a keen interest in the proceedings, but the ferocious Sir Balthasar's eyes blazed with admiration, and he took the three steps that would bring him in front of Molly, went to one knee, and grasped her right hand and kissed it. He rose again, now looking as embarrassed as so tigerish a man could look, bowed, and said, "God and Mary with you, Madam," to a ragged chorus of "Amen" from Sir Jehan and Sir Odinell, and the other knights and men-at-arms within earshot.

Molly, that pagan, just nodded politely. "I thank you, gentlemen." And then: "Nemain!"

She strode down to the forefront of the Norman line. To Turlough of Armagh she said, "Greeting, Master Turlough. I accept her challenge."

The bard looked at her keenly. "Swear now to me."

"I swear by She Whom I swear by, the Mórrígan, to abide by these terms."

"Prepare yourself," said the bard, turning to go.

"A moment," said Molly. "Has she sworn to you, and by Whom?"

He turned back. "She has sworn to me. They are the Tribe of Death, and she has sworn to me by Death Himself, and I have accepted her oath."

"We await your signal," said Molly, and here came Nemain, driving the chariot down through the Norman ranks. Molly took her place, arranged the javelins in their chariot-side cylinder, and stood watching the bard as he walked down to the midpoint of the battlefield.

He signaled to the Hebridean queen: *She has agreed.* Then he stood still, waiting till both queens should be ready.

Chapter 17

FROM BEHIND THE METALLIC WALL of gallowglasses rolled the chariot with Queen Ferelith and her driver, a burly man who wore no armor, only a belted tunic; his moustaches were so long that they were braided, and hung below his chin, and each was weighted with a gold ring. A pattern of knotwork covered his right arm from elbow to wrist; on his cheek was tattooed a triquetra, a symbol of his three queens.

Ferelith was herself also clad in traditional style, without armor, a tunic to the knee and a cloak, echoing Molly and Nemain's attire. She rode in an elaborately painted car, with knotwork borders below the handrail, and spokes painted red and white alternately. A gray horse, a black horse, were hitched to the draw bar: large handsome brutes, with elaborate cheekpiece ornaments of red enamel and gold.

By contrast Molly's chariot was drab and utilitarian—it had been hidden away for years and there was no time for decoration, but it had been repaired and greased and the harness was sound. The two brown mares who drew it were unremarkable, but well trained and in perfect health.

Each queen was now in station before her host, and midway stood the bard Turlough. He looked at Molly, and she raised her right hand, clenched into a fist; he turned, and looked toward the queen of the Uí Bháis, and she did the same. Satisfied that both were ready, he signaled the beginning of combat by the simple expedient of walking off to one side, leaving the long green slope and the level green field to the two chariots.

Nemain snapped the reins and the two mares surged forward; down below, the charioteer did the same, and his horses leaped to obey. They thundered toward each other, Nemain moving somewhat faster, because she was going downslope. As they neared, Queen Ferelith drew a javelin from her chariot's weapon-cylinder, as Molly did from hers. Two arms went back in unison; two javelins were cast at almost the same moment. Molly and Ferelith raised angled shields, and both javelins skittered away into the field.

The traditional practice was for each chariot to ride to the opposite limit of the field, turn, and charge toward the opponent again, but the Uí Bháis charioteer came about almost immediately, a turn that he made as sharp as possible, so that now, upslope from Molly's chariot, he was driving down at their unprotected backs.

A great shout arose from Molly's army, Hob among

them. They were banging sword against shield, and Nemain looked back and realized their peril. She pulled the mares into a turn, as sharp as she dared; she pushed the brake on and off and on and off, so that the chariot, wheels locked, began a sideways slide on the dewy grass, a perilous maneuver. Nemain pulled at one set of reins to slow the left-hand mare and snapped the other to urge on the mare on the right, the chariot sliding, sliding sideways—had they hit a rock they were doomed—and then they were around and running back straight at the Hebridean chariot, having made the turn in a tighter radius than anyone would have believed possible. There was a moment when Hob thought that all would die right then, the horses running full tilt at one another, Nemain not swerving in the least, and then the charioteer's courage failed him or his sense saved him—in either case, he pulled his team over to the right at the very last instant.

Both Molly and Ferelith again cast javelins, but with the chariots rocking and swaying from such violent dodging motions, both spears went far astray. They flew past each other, the light cars bouncing and tilting on the occasional rock half-buried in the soil.

They came around again, this time in wider arcs, and leaped forward. The two queens, each with a third javelin, did not throw this time, but stabbed with them, leaning over the rails toward each other; each blocking with her targe. Just before the chariots came together, Hob thought to see a silver flicker between them.

They continued on away from one another, running toward opposite ends of the field. The Uí Bháis chariot was coming toward Molly's side of the field and Molly was approaching the gallowglasses. Hob saw the charioteer slowly bend forward, as though to observe the space between the horses' tails and the chariot front, then he leaned further and lay upon the rail, and Queen Ferelith quickly reached over and took the reins from his opening hand and he slid down onto the chariot floor and off the back, rolling and bouncing a bit, dead, with Nemain's dagger hilt protruding from his chest.

Queen Ferelith drove back a third of the way. Down at the far end, Nemain had turned the chariot, ready for another charge. The queen of the gallowglasses tied off the reins to the chariot rail and set the brake; the horses stood still, as they had been trained. Ferelith took off her targe and threw it away. Then she drew from the chariot-side weapon cylinder a two-handed gallowglass ax. She was a big woman, but they were big men, and this was a somewhat shorter, somewhat lighter version of the standard gallowglass sparth ax.

She stepped off the back of the chariot and walked a bit down the hill, past her horses. She raised her ax in her right hand, and in a voice that rang through the valley, shouted a long speech directed toward Molly and Nemain down in front of the gallowglass line. Hob's Irish was far from perfect, and this was not Irish but the related Scottish Gaelic, and further distorted by the harsh Norse Gael accent.

Bróccan stood beside him. He turned to the smith. "What does she say, man?"

"She calls a challenge to *Banríon* Maeve: weapon to weapon, hand to hand, queen to queen."

Sir Jehan, up on his destrier, spoke in an undertone, the muttering voice one uses to urge on a horse in a race one watches from afar. "Run her down, Madam; for Jesus's sake, run her down."

But Molly, after a brief consultation with her granddaughter, stepped back and down from the two-wheeled car. Nemain handed her a short stabbing spear and with this she advanced upslope toward Ferelith. Nemain set the brake and went to stand by the mares' heads, holding them by the bridles.

When Molly was perhaps ten paces away Ferelith whirled up the ax and gave a shrill ululating war cry, and then ran full speed at Molly. The ax came down in a flashing arc, and had Molly taken it full force on her shield arm, it might have broken bone, but she angled her targe so subtly that the axhead slid along the surface and plunged to the earth in front of Molly's feet.

Hob's heart was pounding; he was gripping the pitted iron pommel of his war dagger as though he would crush it. This was worse than being in battle himself, standing here watching Molly fight a woman perhaps two decades younger; perhaps more.

He expected Ferelith to be off balance, or the axhead to be stuck for a fatal moment in the earth, but the Uí Bháis queen slid her hands down the shaft and continued the motion forward, twirling the ax butt upward to aim a vicious blow at Molly's face. But Molly leaped sideways, jumping from one foot to the other, and the wooden club whipped past her ear, doing no harm. Molly leaped back another step, and her spear, held overhand in the Irish manner, midway along the shaft, licked out and just kissed Ferelith's thigh. At once a stream of red, not overlarge, ran down the foreign queen's inner leg.

Queen Ferelith stepped back two quick paces to give her a moment's freedom from Molly's spearpoint, and whirled the ax over her head and around again level with Molly's waist, the ax humming with the speed of its passage through the air, a killing blow if ever it landed. But Molly raised her spear high while performing something like a bow, so that her waist was moved just out of the path of the blade; and as the gallowglass queen followed through, Molly stabbed not her opponent but the axhead itself. Hob could hear the *clank* of metal on metal as Molly banged into the axhead, augmenting the force of the Hebridean queen's swing, so that the ax was nearly pulled from her hands.

Ferelith, somewhat off balance, checked the gone-wild swing and began to pull the ax back up over her head for another roundabout killing stroke; and while the foreign queen was doing that, Molly put the spearpoint solidly into the smooth white expanse of her throat. Molly sprang back, ripping the spear out, and Ferelith began to choke and cough, blood running into her lungs.

But the gallowglass code affected contempt for death, and, knowing she was dead on her feet, Ferelith yet staggered two steps and brought the ax down toward Molly's head. Molly clapped her other hand onto the spear and held it two-handed above her head. The ax severed it, but that took all remaining force from the blow, and the weapon wobbled in a shaky arc down to the grass, and a moment later the tall grim queen followed it down. Her strong right hand remained clenched on the haft of the ax; her left clutched a handful of grass and pulled it free, a last grip of Erin; then all movement ceased. Queen Ferelith was dead.

From the ironclad ranks of the gallowglasses came a deep-throated roar, an eerie mix of rage and grief. Yet they did not break ranks, held by their pledge and their rigid discipline. By contrast, the ranks of Molly's army, disparate as they were—Irish, Norman English, Welsh—were as though by common consent silent, almost respectful, at the sight of this strangest of duels, this bloody sacrament, an echo of some dim past, when goddesses strove for the control of ancient tribes in the billowing pearl-tinged mists of deep time.

Molly went to the fallen queen, stooped, held her hand beneath the shattered throat, and stood up with a palmful of blood in her cupped hand. She ran one hand over the other, washing them in Ferelith's blood. Then she drew a white linen cloth from inside her cloak and dried her hands. The cloth, now soaked in crimson patches, she held up till the breeze that ever came breathing in from the Western Ocean lifted it in her hand, and she released it, and it blew away with its burden: the heart's blood of the queen of the Uí Bháis.

Chapter 18

Turlough walked from the spot, off to the side of the battlefield, whence he had observed the combat. He went down, walking with the long easy strides of the wandering bard, to the grim gallowglass line, now utterly silent and standing motionless in perfect lines. He stopped short of the front row, and an older gallowglass came out from the ranks. Hob could see them conferring; it seemed to be drawn out, although when he thought back on it later, he realized that it had been brief—the suspense of waiting to see if they would honor their agreement had made it seem longer.

The gallowglass turned and called orders; six men detached themselves from the ranks, and the little party walked upslope, the Hebrideans moving with a heavy formality that seemed to convey their sorrow. Even for this brief journey the gallowglasses moved in formation: two lines of three men, marching behind the older man, who proved to be their constable, as their commander was known.

Molly awaited them by Ferelith's body. The men came up to her, and Turlough said, "I am witness. Here is the gallowglass constable; make your arrangements."

Molly said nothing for a moment, but only examined the older Hebridean closely. "You were not the constable when first the Uí Bháis came here, surely?" said Molly, for this was not the man she had seen in the Beekeeper's water mirror.

"Nay, Madam," said the constable. "He has died, killed in a cattle raid some years agone."

This disposed of one more target for Molly's sworn vengeance, and one more obstacle to the resolution of the conflict. "Will you remove, then?" said Molly.

"They must," said Turlough, "or I will write such a satire that they will perish of it." The words of a bard could curse, and kill, and cause a person to be banished.

"Give us a day to inform our remaining queen, *Banríon* Nathaira," said the constable in a subdued voice, "and a day to ready the ships and shift our goods into them, and a day to depart. We will remove in three days."

" 'Tis acceptable. But if your remaining queen commands you to stay?"

Turlough made as if to speak, but the constable forestalled him. "We have given our word to depart, Madam; we have sworn by our ancestor, Death Himself."

And with that, he signaled to the squad he had brought

with him, and they placed Queen Ferelith tenderly in her chariot, and then retrieved the body of her charioteer and put him in beside her, and led the horses back down the hill, one man leading the horses, two men walking on each side of the chariot, a hand to the rail, and a man following, to ensure that the bodies should not slip from the open back.

Turlough touched his heart to Molly, who nodded, and strode away to the east, his harp slung to his back, and he came to the beginning of the woodland, and went in under the trees, and so left their sight.

Chapter 19

Molly's army camped in the fields outside the rath while the usurpers prepared to leave. Despite a general wariness on the part of the Normans, Molly was sure there would be no further resistance. She felt the word of the gallowglass constable was honest, and she was rarely wrong about such judgments, and on the strength of it a detail was sent for Macha Redmane and her nurse, back at Castle Dunlevin, and she arrived the next day, to much hugging and kissing from her parents and Molly. Even stolid Jack was moved to give her a hug, careful of his strength, and Sweetlove alternated between exuberance and a certain amount of jealous whining while Jack made much of Redmane.

• • •

The gallowglasses and their squires and their dependents marched out of Molly's rath, heading west toward the switchback path down to the water's edge; the Norman knights lined both sides of the gates and out into the road for a short distance, saluting as their foes filed away. Partly it was to do honor to such ferocious adversaries, and partly, as Roger remarked to Jack and Hob, because "Sir Jehan wants to make sure there's no fucking surprises up those iron sleeves."

But in the event, the departure occurred on schedule, near the end of the third day. The constable had informed Molly that Queen Nathaira would not come with them, nor would she contest possession of the land any more, but only wished to live quietly in her cave with her cats.

"Aye, and I'm sure there's a wolf somewhere who only wants to live quietly among the sheep," said Nemain acidly.

"She is scheming something," said Molly. "But even if she were not, I would not let her live, after what she did to my daughter and to my people. We will come to grips with her, and that very soon. For now, let us purify the rath of this filth, and set all in order. Then we will move against her when all is ready."

From the cliff edge Hob and Jack watched the birlinns sail out past the large rocks that jutted from the water here and there, a short distance from the front of the cliffs, the waves smashing in a welter of white foam and spray against their westward sides. The Hebrideans, expert sailors, stood out to sea for some way. One of the birlinns was towing two boats: one with their dead queen and another with the lesser slain. The birlinns struck their sails; the ships lost way; oars were run out and they maintained their position with intermittent bouts of rowing.

From the towing birlinn, torches were dropped overside into the two boats, which had been prepared in some way, for at once they flowered into towering flames, a column of thick smoke forming above, to be shredded by the sea breezes. The two funeral vessels were cut loose, and began, impelled by the relentless swells of the Western Ocean, to drift slowly back to Ireland, but long before they could be driven ashore they had burned to the waterline and disintegrated into ash and splinter.

When both had been consumed, the Hebrideans shipped their oars and raised sail. They turned south, aiming eventually to round the tip of Erin. Hob watched the sails diminish, dwindling in the distance, and then they passed behind a headland, and disappeared. A faint haze still hung over the water for a while, then it, too, vanished in the wind.

A report reached Hob many years later, brought back by pilgrims, of an attempt by a clan of gallowglasses—surely the Uí Bháis, by the descriptions—to carve a home from the coast of southern Spain. The king of Granada came down with his army: his cavalry mounted on their beautiful and ornately caparisoned horses, his spearmen with graceful calligraphic banners fluttering from their glittering lance-heads, his war musicians with their small kettledrums and their deep-toned horns. The gallowglasses made their stand, mail and axhead glinting in the remorseless Andalusian sun; the Moors overwhelmed them; and the Tribe of Death were known no more.

CHAPTER 20

ONE DAY AFTER THE DEPARTURE of the gallowglasses, Sir Jehan formed a burial party for the knights and men-at-arms slain in the battle. There was no Christian hallowed ground, no church, no clergy, in Molly's clan holdings: the nearest churches were the chapels at St. Mary's priory and at Castle Dunlevin. Wandering missionaries who came to Molly's rath were treated with courtesy, but found the Ó Cearbhaills intractable; preaching fell on deaf ears, and soon such missionaries would decide to resume their travels, seeking less stony ground on which to sprinkle their seeds.

And so the bodies of the fallen were to be loaded onto wains, draped with battle standards, and conveyed south. Sir Jehan, Sir Odinell, and Sir Balthasar, as well as a small party of knights and men-at-arms from both Castle Blanchefontaine and Castle Chantemerle, made up the escort. Hob—Sir Robert—was, though technically Molly's vassal, an informal member of the Blanchefontaine family. Some of the knights who had been killed were vassals of Sir Jehan or of Sir Odinell but not household knights at either castle, and some of the younger household knights were but slightly familiar to Hob; nor had he known any of the slain men-at-arms. But he had known the quiet Sir Walter, parsimonious with speech, since Hob was a boy, and he felt a great deal of grief at his passing. In addition, he owed the sponsorship of his knighthood to Sir Jehan and especially to his mentor, the savage Sir Balthasar, who had actually knighted him.

So it was that he mounted Iarann in the wide field inside the Ó Cearbhaill rath that in a Norman castle would be called a bailey, and waited, the summer sun already making him uncomfortable under the padded gambeson and the mail hauberk, for the wains to form up, and for the men-at-arms forming the rearguard to close ranks behind the second wain. The three senior knights, himself, and two junior knights were the vanguard. The horses were moving slightly in place, eager to be in motion, the knights swaying in their saddles. There was a strong smell of leather, of horse, of the oil that coated the links of mail; over all these were the gusts of salt air: the breath of the nearby ocean.

At last the guards hauled the big leaves of the rath gates open, and Sir Jehan turned his horse into the way; the other knights followed, then the wains, then the company of men-at-arms, Ranulf commanding them and Roger calling cadence.

Molly and Nemain and the other women of the rath lined both sides of the gate and set up a keening for the dead that Hob could hear far into the distance. The pagan Irish had washed their dead, and would spend a day and a night keening and lamenting, and then wrap them in the *es léine*, the death-shirt, and bury them in a grove set aside for that purpose.

Up the Norman party toiled, through the pass that led through the peaks called the Mórrígan, and on past the plashed hedges that had so nearly defeated them. The knights wore mail, for there was a great deal of unrest here in the West: bandits, clan warfare, and the like, and it was best to be prepared for ambush.

A long day's travel brought them to the priory of St. Mary's. The bodies were given into the care of the monks, and the escort dined in the refectory. A messenger was sent to Castle Dunlevin; presently Sir Maurice joined them, for Sir Jehan and Sir Odinell were old friends of his, and some of the fallen knights were known to him as well. Late in the evening the men-at-arms retired to sleep, but the knights, having rested briefly, gathered in the chapel to keep vigil, Hob among them.

They knelt and prayed for much of the night, varying their position occasionally by standing, while Prior Patrick, facing them, led them in prayer; his fingers, long, thin, somewhat swollen at the joints, endlessly cycled through the carved wooden beads of his paternoster. The dim chapel, the darkened windows, the handful of candles casting moving shadows of the praying men, black against gray stone, the faint scent of incense from earlier masses, the prior's droning tenor, the bass rumble of the knights' responses: hour by hour these cast a spell over Hob, till fatigue and repetition induced a mood of mixed sorrow and exaltation, so that the faint lightening of the windowpanes at dawn, and then the full burst of glorious sunlight striking the colored glass, seemed to convey some deep-heart meaning—profound, holy, impossible to articulate.

The bodies were brought in, and the priory chaplain, Father Andrew, said the funeral mass. Absolution and communion were given, and a procession formed, sturdy monks carrying the bodies wrapped in winding sheets, down the central aisle, out the double doors and around and through the lich gate to the little churchyard, followed by the knights.

The sextons had been at work at first light, and the bodies were lowered into the new-dug graves. Prayer was continuous throughout; the graves were filled and temporary marker stones placed, and then it was done. They turned away, Hob crossing himself, still seeing Sir Walter the first few nights Molly's troupe had stayed at Castle Blanchefontaine: pleasant, stolid, but saying very little. There had been a chess tournament, which Molly of course had won, and he had been Molly's first victim. Even as she had destroyed his forces he had said but little, elbow on table and hand covering his mouth, but he had bowed to her at the conclusion and acknowledged defeat with real admiration.

They went in to breakfast, but talk was subdued. Soon thereafter the company began re-forming for the journey home. Hob went to see Prior Patrick. The prior's face was somewhat drawn from his all-night prayer session, and at the sight of Hob, who frightened him, his expression deepened into one of real woe.

But Hob hastened to reassure him. He drew forth the pouch of silver that Molly had provided him for the purpose, and said, "Brother Patrick, pray take this for all your kindness to us and to our beasts, and be assured that the Sieur de Blanchefontaine and the Sieur de Chantemerle are grateful for your reception of their dead; I believe they will wish to express it to you directly."

The prior accepted the pouch, his eyebrows rising as he felt the weight of it. He put the bag upon his desk without looking in it. "I thank you, Sir Robert. Do you wish us to continue our care of your livestock?"

"Why, no; pray have your grooms bring them forth, with rope leads: we will bring them home with us."

OUT IN THE ROAD, mounted on Iarann, Hob waited beside Sir Balthasar while Sir Jehan and Sir Odinell said their farewells to Prior Patrick and left their gifts for the priory. Here came two grooms, one carrying a wooden hoop to which were tied three lead ropes of varying lengths. The ropes were fastened to the bridles on Molly's three draft animals. Hob accepted the hoop and fixed it to the right side of his saddle.

Then he dismounted and walked around Iarann, one hand to the destrier's neck to let him know where he was. Milo came forward a few steps to meet him and put his large soft muzzle against the unyielding mail on Hob's chest and made ludicrous snuffing sounds as he tried to catch Hob's scent through the armor. Hob put his arms around the ox's neck and patted and slapped him a bit, murmuring in Milo's ear. Then he went down the line to the other two beasts, scratching Mavourneen behind the ears, stroking the mare Tapaigh's neck. It did not occur to Hob, so much time had he spent over the years with these three, that it might be behavior more suited to a goat-boy than the feared Sir Robert.

One of the younger knights from Castle Chantemerle looked at another, the beginnings of mirth tugging at the corners of his mouth. Then he noticed that his comrade was looking ahead, stone-faced, and he turned and met the basilisk glare of Sir Balthasar, who said nothing but looked at him steadily. The young knight suddenly found that he needed to check the buckles on his saddlebags, and busied himself therewith.

And then they were on the road again. To the knights, hardened by years of campaigning, a missed night's sleep was to be taken in stride, although at least one of the younger knights was dozing in the saddle. The Norman saddles, with their high cantles, made it easy to stay in place while half-awake, and the knights kept to a walk to accommodate the marching men-at-arms.

Milo and the other two mismatched draft animals ambled along, tethered on Hob's right side, and he remembered when he used to jest to himself about Milo being his destrier, the warhorses so called because they were always led on the right or dexter side. And now he had his own big gray Iarann moving beneath him. The day was sunny but cool, and he felt his spirits begin to lift after the sorrow of the funeral.

Up the rise and into the pass between the mountains, Sir Jehan pulling back to ride stirrup to stirrup with Hob. He gestured to the narrowing path, the mountains on either hand crowding in: "Sir Robert, I believe your queen would do well to stretch a wall across this gap, with a fortified . . . fortified gatehouse; I have the very builder for it at home, and I would be pleased to send him to her."

"I will so inform her, Sir Jehan," said Hob. "Certes, I believe she is interested in refashioning the rath in stone: having seen Norman strongholds, and Norman siege engines, she feels that in this case the old ways may not be best."

"I will speak to her . . . speak to her myself, then, if this be the case," said Sir Jehan. "I thought . . . I thought to approach you, and have you suggest it to her, for . . . I did not want to seem to, to . . . slight her ancient home."

THERE WAS THE USUAL raucous welcome from the Irish gateguards, friendly but not deferential—the Irish kerns having a tradition, similar to those among the Welsh and the Scots, of speaking freely to one's chieftain, the result of a tribal society, where everyone was related in some way. The column had barely entered the gates, crossing the grassy expanse toward the stables, when it was swarmed by excited children and youths, everyone talking at once, and here came Molly and Nemain, and Jack carrying Redmane on his shoulders so she could see better above the crowd. Hob could not see Sweetlove for the crowd, but he could hear her high-pitched enthusiastic barking.

He swung down from the saddle and was immediately caught in an embrace by Nemain, and Macha Redmane, one hand gripping Jack's hair, leaned down for a kiss. If having a hank of his hair pulled distressed Jack, he gave no sign. Molly was greeting and welcoming the senior knights, and eventually the knights' horses were handed off to grooms and the men-at-arms dismissed, and the whole crowd drifted toward the great hall. Hob, though, wanted to stable Iarann himself—he did not like entrusting his animals to others, although sometimes it was inevitable.

The wooden ring was divested of its lead ropes, and Nemain descended upon Mavourneen with glad cries and caresses, and Jack gave Redmane Tapaigh's lead rope and they started toward the stables, Sweetlove running in rapid circles around them, barking with unfocused excitement. Hob had Iarann's reins in his left hand and had to go stooping for Milo's lead rope, since the moment the ox had been untied he began to wander off, grazing, seduced by the long sweet Irish grass.

Into the long cool aisle of the rath's stables he went, placing Iarann in one stall and Milo in the other. Hob took care to spend time with the big destrier, gray as iron—*iarann* in Irish—and already had much the same bond with the horse as he did with Milo.

It was more than affection: a knight must have confidence in and loyalty from his mount, since they protected each other's lives in the midst of those who would kill them if they could. When the horse had been divested of its saddle and blanket, and rubbed down, and fed and watered and generally stroked and told of its virtues in the murmuring voice that people use to beloved animals, Hob went to the next stall and repeated most of the process with Milo.

"I wonder who Daddy is talking to in there." Nemain's voice, outside the stall door. "There's no one else therein save that ox. Surely the great Sir Robert would not be chattering away to an ox, would he?"

Amusement, exasperation, love—he swung open the stall door and there she stood in a characteristic pose, leaning against the wall with arms folded and an expression of teasing mischief, Redmane beside her with one hand bunched in Nemain's skirts.

"Nemain . . ." Hob began, but Redmane forestalled him. She looked up at her mother and said, quite seriously, "Daddy has to talk to Milo because Milo's little on the inside although he's big on the outside, and he's Daddy's baby. I'm his baby, too."

Nemain heard this with delight. "Why, thank you for explaining that, treasure of my heart! And here I thought the dreaded Robert the Englishman was slipping into an early dotage, but I see that there is quite the explanation for—"

There was only one defense against Nemain's teasing—once started she could go on for a long while—and he took it, Redmane clapping her hands at Daddy's long kiss.

"Hob—" said Nemain hoarsely, a little flushed. Then she looked at Redmane, standing there like the audience at a puppet show, and thought better of it. "Nay, 'twill wait. Let us eat—you must be tired and hungry."

He took Nemain's hand and Redmane's hand, and off they went across the grass of the rath yard, into the wooden tower and through the guardroom into the great hall. Here there was some confusion—the rath was still being cleaned and set in the order that Molly desired—but gradually the returning knights were sitting down amid a chaos of kerns and farmers and their families, children running here and there, and a young man in a corner by himself, playing surprisingly beautiful airs on a *claírseach.*

Hob sat on a bench, swaying with weariness, and let Nemain feed him and bring him drink, while Redmane's chatter washed over him, the clatter and hum of the crowd as a background, and somewhere the harp singing, the voice of a solitary angel.

Chapter 21

Hob awoke from a small sleep with a start; he found himself in their new bedchamber, alone. He became aware, not for the first time, of the subtle pervasive scent of the woods used in the log-built rath. The walls, rubbed and polished with beeswax, gave off a faint but sweet perfume of the wood itself mixed with a honey accent from the wax; the wood was golden in the light of two candle lanterns that hung on chains from the ceiling. The quarters Molly had assigned to them were up on the second level of the central wooden keep, and the window, the shutters partly open, admitted the sound of insects shrilling in the grass of the bailey; the hoot, several times repeated, of an owl; and now and then human voices, the words indistinct.

He stretched, and Nemain came in from the adjoining room with a pitcher of cold water and a small jug of the *uisce beatha*. She gave him a goblet—Spanish glass from the Galway merchant houses—and poured a measure of the fiery spirit, and filled another goblet with pure water from the rath's excellent wells.

Hob hardly remembered lying down. The day's journey south, the sleepless night of vigil, the day's journey home, had tired him to the bone. He had eaten a small amount and retired, and slept for a time, and now was awake, the evening still young.

Nemain sat on the side of the bed. "I've put Redmane to bed. She was aglow—the new home, the new children to befriend. Then down goes her head to the pillow and off to her dreams. Just like her daddy."

"Hum," said Hob, still not quite awake but sipping at the *uisce* and gradually becoming more animated. "And where is Herself? She was not in the hall, and I have not seen her since we came through the gates."

"She is with Sir Tancred, and is nursing him with her own hands." Sir Tancred of Castle Blanchefontaine, a widower perhaps twenty or twenty-five years Molly's junior, had taken a blow in the side from a gallowglass ax that had riven his mail and his gambeson and opened a wound that, although not harming any major organ, had left a gash nine inches long and a half-inch deep.

Nemain hitched herself a little closer and took the goblet from Hob, took a sip, gave it back. "Surely you remember, just before Fox Night so many years agone, we women singing to the harps, and Sir Tancred fascinated by Herself, and losing his heart to her, him who'd lost his wife two years before, and wasn't he devoted to Herself from then on?"

"He was? How do you come to know these things, wife?" It was usually "wife" and "husband" when they were not being serious with each other, "Nemain" and "Hob" when they were, and "my lady" and "Sir Robert" when strangers were about.

"Everyone knows it," said Nemain.

"Well, but . . . *I* didn't know it."

"Husbands don't know anything. Dame Aline told me, how he was lovestruck and writing sonnets and such, and even Roger's Lucinda was telling Herself and me of it."

"And so she's tending him? He must have joy of that."

"Well, there he is, helpless as a babe, and she's undressing him and washing him and he's blushing and tongue-tied—no sonnets now—I had this partly from Herself, she could see he was ill at ease, and partly from that lass Fionnuala who's helping Herself when I'm busy with the bairn. And so Herself is putting him at ease, joking with him and complimenting him on his bravery and such, and sure he relaxes and now they're grand friends, laughing together—when he's not wincing—and jesting as though they were together from the cradle."

Hob had been leaning on an elbow, sipping at his drink. Now he sat up and swung his legs over the side of the bed, the beginning of a frown just forming. Nemain took advantage of the moment to steal another sip of his drink; then she added more *uisce* from the jug.

"She's never going to leave Jack for Tancred, is she?"

Molly and Jack had been lovers since he had known them, and Molly had turned down many men in those years because of Jack.

Nemain laughed. "Nay, she's but kindly disposed toward Sir Tancred, whatever he may feel for his part. And in truth, Sir Tancred may be seeing himself as one of those lovers in the romances from the troubadours, all pure and chaste love. For I think he's not feeling himself her equal, and will be content to be her admirer."

She grew more serious. "Herself, whatever their differences in station, is dead faithful to Jack—she started by lusting after him, and now she loves him, as she says, 'unto death.' She's told me this, Hob, and I've never seen her more earnest. He's never as wise as she, nor does she look to him for advice—he's her soldier, as 'twere, and she his queen, but she'd never leave him. And she's had a mort of offers, and turned down every one. You wouldn't know it to look at them—for in what is he her equal?—but there 'tis."

Hob considered this, and it pleased him. Molly was the closest thing to a mother that he'd had, and Jack was like a favorite uncle, and while he knew they were close, he'd often wondered with a tinge of worry, because of the difference in their station and their abilities, if she'd tire of Jack.

"Well," he said now with a grin, "he's not her equal in wealth, or wit, or war, but I suppose Jack could pick up much heavier things than Herself."

"'Tis true," said Nemain, "but you know what I mean. Think you: if she decided to kill him for any reason, he would be dead. The reverse is not true."

Hob had another drink. "You have the right of it, and I believe 'tis true of us as well."

Nemain stood up and let her shift fall to the floor, her pale skin glowing in the lantern-light. She slipped in beside him. "Then ware how you behave, husband."

He kissed her, and then kissed her again. "Pray spare me, my queen," he murmured.

She turned on her back and stretched, her arms up above her head, the covers slipping to her waist. He was leaning on his elbow beside her. She looked up at him, her green eyes alight with the old mischief he remembered, the teasing child he grew up with, the laughing bride.

"Make me scream, husband, and I may let you live."

He looked at her, half in amusement and half in delight. "As you command, my queen," he murmured, reaching for her, bending to her kiss.

Chapter 22

After Molly and Nemain had spent three days purifying their home, with burning of spices and incense and chanting and some things from which Hob and the menfolk had been excluded, the Ó Cearbhaills had taken formal possession of the rath, and the more mundane work had begun: cleaning the rooms and bringing in fresh firewood and reassigning dwellings and bringing in food from the farms around and the like. After two weeks of intensive activity, and with many things to be done in the year ahead, they were ready for a feast, and the Normans, who had been camped in the fields outside, were happy to celebrate the return to power of *Banríon* Maeve, and thus the discharge of at least some of the debt the knights owed Molly and her family, for saving not one but two castles' inhabitants from singularly unpleasant fates.

The bulk of the tribesmen who were attached to the court—the household kerns, the clan officials such as the bards and the treasurer and the stablemaster—lived in cottages within the palisade walls of the rath. More of the clan lived in outlying villages or on isolated farms. Molly's immediate family lived on the upper floors of the wooden keep. The great hall took up most of the ground floor of that tower, and people came and went freely, ate communal meals there, conducted business and litigation, Molly or Nemain presiding, or came to watch the conduct of business or litigation.

The arrangement was the opposite of a Norman castle's in that Molly's chair of office was set, not on a dais at one end of the hall, but at floor level, in the center, so that she was surrounded by her kin at their tables, seated on benches. Here she dealt with clan concerns for a certain period each day; here she took her meals; here in the evenings she sang or heard singers and harpers or listened, usually with someone's child drowsing on her ample lap, to the itinerant storytellers who visited the rath for an evening's meal, a night's lodging. Traveling bards such as Turlough of Armagh would not only chant the histories of the great tribes of Erin, the deeds of heroes, or praise poems to Maeve herself, but would also bring news of events throughout Erin and beyond.

Jack was at one point drinking with some of the Blanchefontaine men-at-arms and Hob had joined them. Talk turned to the differences between Sir Jehan's castle and this rath, and Roger had remarked on the central location of Molly's chair. "Your Norman grandee wouldn't have people he didn't know mucking about behind him. I'm thinking it'd be a great help to some traitor, him pulling a big fucking knife and you with your back to him."

Hob had thought about this, and said, "She is seated among folk who are her kinsmen, not vassal nor servant nor serf, and were someone to attempt to work her a mischief, others nearby would thwart it. Also, think you, Roger, these women have their Art, and can sense all manner of things we cannot."

Ranulf said, "He's right, lad. Queen Maeve is no fool, and I'm sure she knows what she's about." He and Roger had developed a heartfelt fondness for the *uisce beatha,* and this night neither of them had stinted himself. He looked about somewhat blearily. " 'Tis a pleasant place, and not so yes-my-lord and no-my-lord as 'tis back in England. A man could be happy here, were it not for the people all speaking fucking gibberish as they do—no offense to your people, Sir Robert, but not a word of decent English do they know."

Hob was thinking of something that Molly said from time to time, and now he said, "Things are different in Erin, that's all."

Roger was watching a woman with a mane of black hair like that of his Lucinda back at Blanchefontaine; she was one of a group of younger women clustered about Nemain, questioning their young queen about life in England and about her adventures, making much of Redmane, and the like. Now, chin in hand and elbow on the table, sipping steadily at his cup, he said, "Yon's a comely maid."

Ranulf gave a bark of laughter. "Do tell us about Lucinda again, lad."

Roger flushed and turned away. "Well, 'twas just that she reminded me of Lucinda, and us so fucking far away."

Ranulf clapped Roger on the shoulder, and Hob poured a bit more into the soldier's cup. "We'll be home soon enough, lad," said Ranulf, "and what a greeting you'll get!"

On the night of the victory feast, the great hall was lit with torches and candles; there was a fire in the hearth to keep away the night chill from the constant ocean winds, and harp music and singing, and venison dishes and mutton and pastries; the stores of ale and *uisce beatha* that the Uí Bháis had perforce to leave behind were broached. There was even imported wine that the usurpers had purchased from the storehouses of the Galway merchants.

Molly and Nemain sang, each playing a *cláirseach*, a harp, as well, and then Hob and Jack resumed their old roles for a bit, Hob on the symphonia and Jack on the bodhran. A young woman, Sciath, stout, pretty, with the black hair and blue eyes so typical of the Celts, sang a lament in so pure and ethereal a voice that the Normans were silent as stones till she finished.

Afterward slim Sir Geoffrey, a knight from Castle Chantemerle, sang some troubadour verses, which, though incomprehensible to most of the Irish at the banquet, were well received because of the knight's melodious voice, because of good fellowship, and because of the prodigious amounts of honey beer and barley beer and ale and Spanish wine and *uisce beatha* that had been consumed.

There was little ill behavior, though: raised or angry voices were quelled at a look from Nemain. Once she had to stand at her place and glare down the table, but that was all, and Molly did not even have to do a thing.

"Watch Mommy frightening the drunken kerns," said Hob to his baby queen, his queen baby, cutting portions of venison for Redmane, sitting on his lap. Molly was quite happy, sitting with a large goblet of the *uisce beatha*—for she liked her drink as well as anyone—and occasionally looking about the hall and her people in it, seated to either side of her chair, down the long table and at tables along the wall, and her expression, thought Hob, saying, *At last, at last.*

Later she was deep in consultation with Sir Jehan and Sir Odinell: she wanted to work toward establishing a real Norman castle, of stone instead of wood, that the Ó Cearbhaills might be more secure, and was willing to allow a small Norman settlement nearby, to bring in Norman architects and builders and stoneworkers, and in general to maintain the ties of friendship and aid that she had developed with the knights and their respective castle-folk.

And here was Sir Jehan rising to announce the betrothal of Philip, one of his men-at-arms, to Ciannait, a maid of the Ó Cearbhaills, the groom to be detached from Sir Jehan's service with his blessing, that this might be a symbol of the friendship between the two communities, "and that our Philip may learn the Irish tongue, and be a translator for us when we establish our settlement."

How Philip and Ciannait came to agree to wed was somewhat mysterious, given the language barrier, but Hob leaned over to Jack and said, "I trow Roger has some hand in this, with his new-found joy in marriage."

Molly's big wooden chair was carved from back to foot with interlocking knots from which peered stylized crow heads; the feet were fashioned to resemble cat's paws with claws extended; on the top of the chair back was sculpted a lifelike raven that seemed to be leaning down and speaking to the chair's occupant. On Molly's lap were three of her tribesmen's children, a girl of four summers, a boy perhaps three, and a girl about six. Molly was absently feeding them mouthfuls of honey cake; another girl of perhaps ten leaned against the arm of the chair, listening intently and with an utter lack of comprehension to Molly's conversation with Sir Jehan, whose artificial hand seemed to fascinate her. Tonight, rather than the functional steel battle glove, he wore the beautiful bronze-and-green-gold hand.

The knight, like Roger, was bemused at the great informality of Molly's court, but, as she explained to him, "These are not my tenants, or folk bound to me by law. 'Tis a clan: we are all related, near or far, by blood or marriage."

And of course Sir Jehan found it remarkable that everyone, no matter how old or young, addressed Molly as "Grandmother," and Nemain as "Mother."

"And so even an old . . . an old man . . . he would address Queen Nemain as 'Mother,' no matter the difference in their ages?" asked Sir Jehan.

"And how would you be calling one of your priests, and

he a man two-thirds your age?" she retorted. "Would you not call him 'Father'?"

"Ha!" said Sir Jehan, and lifted his goblet to her. "You have me . . . you have me there, Madam, and 'tis a very clear path to understanding you've shown me. And as I have said many a time—the world is wide, and many things therein."

A few days later Hob and Jack stood at the same spot on the cliff whence they had watched the departure of the Úi Bháis and watched another small fleet of ships depart: the cogs carrying Sir Jehan and Sir Odinell and their vassals, with all their horses and weapons, sailing southward, so to round the southern coast of Ireland and eventually gain the English Channel, bound for the Northumbrian coast.

That night, lying abed in their new chambers, speaking of the departure of Sir Jehan's folk, and of the triumphal feast, with the Normans, the Welsh, and the Ó Cearbhaills all gathered together, Hob said to Nemain, "It was a fine thing to see Herself at ease in her chair of state, and all her people rejoicing with her, and proud of her, and a pile of bairns about her."

She stretched and looked at him with slightly glassy eyes—she had drunk a great deal that night at dinner, and Hob thought she might not have heard him. But after a moment she said in a quiet voice, "She was happy, and so am I, but there is a shadow on this rath. We must deal with that witch queen; she is hanging there like a spider, waiting her chance to rush down upon us with her poison. Herself is concerned, so great an adept is Nathaira. Yet she did not come to the aid of the gallowglasses. 'Tis like a day when the clouds darken and darken the sky: there is no storm yet, but there will be—everyone knows it, everyone."

Part III

THE CRONE

The twilight's gleam is in her eyes,
The night is on her hair

—Joseph Campbell, "My Lagan Love"

Chapter 23

BAD DREAMS ALONG THE COAST. Sheep gone missing, then a cow or two. A young boy, a shepherd, running into his father's cottage, hysterical. A dragon has come up from the sea, climbing the cliffs, clinging with many legs, and paralyzed the big ram with two prongs coming from his head, and backed up again, dragging the ram away, and vanished below the cliff line.

Molly, Queen Maeve, heard these complaints in her hall, seated in her chair of state, holding her daily hearings into the disputes and petitions of her people. Nemain, seated at her right hand, looked darkly at her grandmother.

"'Tis her, Grandmother," she said. "She's begun."

"Aye," said Molly, low enough for it to be between them. "Who else, who else?"

More reports came in: the monster came from the cliffs to the north, where was the witch queen's cave, but low down near the waterline. It had many legs; it seemed to cling to the solid rock; it seized something, paralyzing it, and dragged it back down to its lair.

"Have four horses saddled," said Molly to her castellan, "and have Daire assemble a small escort."

Hob donned mail and a helm, armored gloves and greaves, and saddled Iarann himself. Molly and Nemain had prepared a small leather satchel, filled with their mysteries: Hob knew better than to ask. Jack, who was good with horses—he was gentle with them, and they trusted him—but an awkward rider, heaved himself up into the saddle, slotted his war hammer into a leather loop, and sat rather glumly awaiting the signal to move. When Daire clattered up from the stables with eight of the dashing Irish cavalry behind him—cloaks flying, light spears cocked against their thighs, and wool saddle pads without stirrups instead of the heavy Norman saddles Hob and Jack were using—they were ready to start.

The broad gates swung open, and they trotted out. Daire had kept five men close to his queens, and sent three on ahead as scouts. They turned north on the coast path, and rode for some little time with the cliffs falling away on their left hand, the pressure of the perennial wind from the Western Ocean fluttering their clothes and hair, the muted roar of the waves so far below, breaking on the offshore rocks, crashing in a gout of flung spray against the cliffs, a constant drone in their ears.

There were many small settlements under Molly's jurisdiction, clusters of a few cottages, with a handful of residents. The first two that they came to were unharmed, although the farmers there were frantic at the rumors that had come to them, clustering around their queens and begging for protection. Molly soothed them as best she could, and they fared on northward for a time. The third such hamlet held a scene of horror: no one left alive; a headless woman; two dead children, bloated and blackened by some poison; a cow with some limbs raggedly torn off.

Molly and her family dismounted; Daire's men fanned out to form a rough periphery guard around the hamlet. A track in the dust told of someone dragged to the cliff and over. Hob looked more closely: two rows of parallel lines indicated that someone had dug their fingers into the dirt in a vain attempt to keep from being carried away.

The cottages were in ruins. Walls were shattered, the thatch of the roofs was burst and strewn everywhere, the planks of the floors were painted red with blood. A disembodied foot was half-buried in the ashes of a fireplace; in one room a couple huddled, great wounds in their backs showing what had killed them.

Everywhere were strange round footprints, many of them, with two clawlike piercings accompanying each. Over all was the strangest scent. Hob tried to identify it: partly it smelled of spices, partly it had an organic odor, like a stable. It was not unpleasant, but it was so odd that it began to oppress Hob. He would feel compelled to sniff and identify it, and yet he could not. He dismissed it from his thoughts one moment and then a moment later was testing the air again.

" 'Tis the scent of this monster," said Nemain.

"Aye, but what is it?" said Molly.

They went outside and followed the tracks to the cliff edge. Molly looked north, to where even higher cliffs piled up, rising toward the mountain range behind.

"She has her cave up there, where the higher cliffs are, and it's my thinking that there are passageways from up there to down here where our monster lives. Has she been raising this . . . whatsoe'er it may be . . . all this time, for revenge?"

"Is it here, then, *seanmháthair*?" asked Hob.

"The tracks go straight over, and that eldritch scent is everywhere. . . ."

But now Nemain lifted her head sharply; she looked toward the cliff edge, the vast stretch of water rolling in from the horizon. "Hark!" she said, but all Hob could hear was the muted bellow of the ocean against the foot of the cliffs, the hiss of the wind. Then:

"A drum?" he said.

There was a rattle of quick drumbeats; then a pause, then another.

" 'Tis no drum," said Molly. "Ware the cliff!"

The odor intensified, and then Hob felt his blood chilling. Dimly he was aware of the plunging hooves and frantic cries of the horses behind him as Daire struggled to hold all four of theirs while controlling his own mount. Behind him the Irish riders were cursing as they hauled at their reins, their horses trying to bolt. Hob flicked a glance behind him: Iarann was standing still, but his ears were flat, his lips drawn back from his teeth.

Hob turned back. The scent grew intense. Above the lip of the cliff a nightmare was rearing into view: a head that seemed all mandibles and waving palps; a body of segments, each segment armored in a glossy flexible brown material, and each with a pair of legs. The first segment had two crescent claws that dripped a sinister fluid, and clicked together again and again. The drumbeats were produced by the many legs, more and more as each segment cleared the cliff edge. The multi-jointed legs ended in sucker pads and clinging spikes. It climbed easily, fluidly, sliding up the cliff and onto the land.

Molly and Nemain stepped back sharply, calling to Hob and Jack to come away. But, moved by some instinct to kill that which was so hideous, so out of all nature, the men separated and came at the head from each side. Hob drew his sword as he ran up to it and aimed a two-handed blow at the join of the head to the first segment. The shock of impact ran up through his hands, his wrist, to his forearms, but the sword rebounded from whatever substance this demon thing was made of. It swung around at him, he leaped backward, and the two huge claws slammed together where he had been, amber poison dripping from the hollow tips. Where the drops hit, they smoked in the dust.

While the monster was snapping at Hob, Jack tried to bury the crow-beak of his war hammer in the second segment. He succeeded in making a slight dent in the armored side, but that was all.

"Back now, back now!" roared Molly in a parade-ground voice, and both men, having proved the futility of an attack with ordinary steel, trotted backward, eyes on the demon. For its part, the beast did not seem to see well: there were eyelike structures in its head, made of what seemed to be many little eyes, but not what might be called true eyes. It cast about this way and that, to find where its enemies had got to.

"Mount up, Jack, Hob," snapped Nemain. "'Tis no normal creature; we will deal with it."

She had the leather satchel open and she withdrew a hollow reed, and another; fitted one within the other, thus doubling the length; poured powder in one end, the creature lining up with them and beginning to resume its forward progress. The women were backing up as well and Nemain handed the long hollow reed to Molly, seized the satchel and moved back, back. The whole beast was up on their level now, a being as long as four wagons, each as long as Molly's big wagon.

Molly aimed the reed at the big questing head, and Nemain began a loud rapid chant, the words in an archaic Irish that Hob could not follow. Molly drew a great breath, and blew into the mouthpiece of the reed. From the bell-shaped outlet came a long stream of purple dust, with an iridescent sheen to the billows. It enveloped the thing's head, and immediately a transparent membrane slid up over the compound eyes, the creature gave a hiss like a giant snake, and it shook its head in evident distress.

Then it reared up, segment after segment rising, till a third of its length was up in the air, poison claws threatening, the raised portion anchored to the earth by the two-thirds that stood level.

Hob threw himself into Iarann's saddle, snatched the reins of the women's horses from Daire, and spurred forward to the two queens. Molly and Nemain mounted, and they rode back a little distance and turned again. Jack had managed to remount, albeit awkwardly, and was leaning forward against his horse's neck, stroking it, talking to it, to keep it from stampeding.

The horrid beast dropped back to earth with a dull boom against the dirt, turned in a tight radius, and flowed back over the cliff. They heard the drumming sound, now receding; they were left with the disorienting sensation of being on an empty cliff where a short while ago was a huge dire creature.

A few moments while they considered the fact that everyone was still alive, and then Hob urged Iarann close to the cliff, dismounted again, and dropped prone to the ground. He crept to the edge and peered over. He saw the creature, head down, flowing down the rock like a mountain stream. Perhaps three-quarters of the way down, well above the waterline, it curled into a cave, and out of sight.

Hob remounted, and they rode inland for a while, till the seaside cliffs were out of sight behind a low hill, and drew rein in a little copse of hazel trees. Daire and the other men clustered in a knot about them, some looking back the way they had come.

Hob said to Daire, "Two men to ride back to the top of

this hill here, and keep watch that it does not return." Daire told off the men and they trotted up the hill. The rest sat their horses about their queens, the men white-faced and silent.

Molly said to Nemain, "What shall we do to overcome this monster?"

"But have you not routed it, *seanmháthair*?" said Hob.

Nemain brought her horse around so that she was facing him. "Husband, that powder itself is half-alive, and the chant I'm singing guides it to its prey, and so it should have swarmed into every opening in that thing's body, and killed it within heartbeats. 'Tis in pain, now, and I'm thinking 'twill not be up to more mischief this day, but it should have been dead twice over, and this queen, this Nathaira, has both raised it up to its great size and armored it with some spell. We must find some way to destroy it entirely."

One of Daire's cavalrymen, a man named Bradan, a distant cousin of Molly's, said to Nemain, "Can a demon like this be killed, Little Mother?"

Nemain looked at him. "Did you not recognize it, with its great size? She has not raised it up from some land of demons, she has created it—but not from nothing, not from the seaweed on the rocks. She started with a living creature, and somehow made it grow, and ensorcelled it, but what she's begun with is nought but an Irish centipede, and you are the ants on which it feeds."

As soon as she said it Hob could see it, but the horror of such a thing—and a smooth killer at that—brought to the size of three cottages—was such that everyone just sat and stared at the two queens.

"If it is a living creature, can we not kill it with arrows, or fire?" asked Hob.

"If that were so, the dust would have slain it," said Molly. "There's a horrid mixture of nature and the Art in this, and any weapon against it must also mix the two in equal measure. The wild white bulls of England, could I but bring them here, would fail against it: it is . . . enameled, you might say . . . with sorcery, and yet its physical body is so simple as to be mindless, so that one cannot get a purchase on its will."

"I cannot think what weapon might serve, *seanmháthair*," said Nemain. "I cannot think where to begin."

"Nor I," said Molly. "This is sorcery of the Scottish Isles, and foreign to me, and she a woman of great power, Crone power."

"This is the power that accrues to older women? Did you not say that?" asked Hob.

"'Tis," said Molly. "Though she is not so old as I am, and I am no kitten of the Art, yet it varies from woman to woman, and Nathaira has it in great measure. She overthrew Macha, my daughter, Nemain's mother, and herself an adept of the Art, with no trouble atall, ensorcelling a banquet hall full of our foremost kin."

"Why not seek aid from one older, and one mightier, than she?" asked Hob. "Did you not tell me of the Beekeeper, and she the most ancient woman of the Art?"

Molly and Nemain looked at one another. "There are times when he's thick as yon hazel tree—" said Nemain.

"—and times when he's not," said Molly. "At dawn tomorrow, we'll ride to the vale of the Beekeeper. If yet she lives, she will aid us."

Nemain kneed her horse so that it sidled right up to Iarann, caught Hob's belt and put a foot on top of his foot in the stirrup, so that she could stand up on one leg and so reach him, up on the tall destrier, and reward him with a sound kiss on the lips, right there in the center of all the cavalrymen, and they all grinning now, relieved as they were that something might be done against the monster, and pleased as they were with their dashing little queen.

AS SOON AS THEY PASSED the gates of the Ó Cearbhaill rath, Molly assigned some women and a detail of guards to bring all the children up to the shieling, the buildings where the shepherds and goatherds stayed when tending their flocks in the up-mountain summer pastures to the east. Wains were loaded with the young, and after farewells, some tearful, they departed for safety. "'Twill be one less peril to fret about, and they'll be home as soon as we've destroyed this *arracht,* this monster," said Molly, and though no one was happy with the turn of events, no one wanted the children exposed to danger either.

CHAPTER 24

IT WAS NOT REALLY UNPLEASANT, thought Hob. It was more of a lassitude, a languorous disinclination to undertake anything further, to travel any farther: a feeling of being pleasantly at rest. Iarann seemed also to feel it, for he had stopped without Hob's command. I might have guessed that someone so benevolent as the old woman would use a gentle restraint, Hob thought.

Beside him Molly and Nemain sat their horses quietly; behind him Jack was dismounted, stroking his horse's muzzle, combing its mane with his fingers. He was a man who, deprived of all but the minimum of speech, expressed affection through his hands; when he found himself in proximity to a dog or horse, he would almost always react by caressing or grooming it. And indeed for such a brutal fighter he had a gentle touch. Molly had once, as deep in drink as she allowed herself, spoken unguardedly of his lovemaking to Hob and Nemain: "the strength of a smith and the hand of a harper."

It was cool here in the defile, even on a warm summer day. The steep slopes that climbed to either hand were clad in dense forest, and the path was always in shade except for a brief period at midday.

When some time had passed—not a great amount, but not a short while, either—here came a little goldcrest, appearing from the shadows under the trees upslope on Molly's side. It hovered a moment, as if determining whom to address, and then settled on Molly's horse, right on its crown, near its left ear. The horse flicked the ear in irritation, and the goldcrest gave a little sideways hop to avoid it. Then, cocking its head so that its eye focused on Molly, it launched into a long burst of song, after which it sprang into the air and sped away into the trees.

Even as it began singing Hob felt his drowsy mood dissipate; Iarann snorted and pawed twice at the ground; and Molly said quietly, "Away on."

They rode up and up through the dappled sunshine, birds making the forest on either side ring with piercing cries, with chattering warnings, and with pure warbled song. They reached the crest of the pass and began to descend, the horses leaning back a bit against the slope.

Hob saw a valley that was oval in shape, and so ringed and defended by the cliffs and peaks of the encircling mountains that it appeared to have been constructed with walls.

Half the valley was left to forest, the canopies of the trees forming a green ceiling that concealed the ground below from his gaze. The other half had small fields marked off, planted to various vegetables and grains. Nearer to the valley wall, an orchard showed orderly rows of trees. Against the rock itself nestled a thatch-roofed cottage, and in front of this, but to one side, was a beeyard with neat rows of skeps.

They reached the valley floor and followed a path between dog-rose hedges. These were loosely planted, and certainly not plashed: there was no threat of an ambush here. Indeed, thought Hob, a gradual mood of well-being, a sense of safety and health, was beginning to permeate his soul. They rode at a walk up to the cottage yard.

A goat, grazing along in the aisles between the apple trees, raised its head and bleated at them once, twice, and here, coming briskly from among the humming rows of woven-basket skeps, was the *Bean na beacha,* the Woman of the Bees, a tiny sun-browned woman, shorter even than Nemain, with hair white as washed wool and small capable hands.

Behind her came an enormous wolfhound. The shaggy head was on a level with the Beekeeper's own, and the dog surely outweighed her. It watched the newcomers keenly, but made no sound, and hovered near the wee old woman all the time. Hob thought to himself that it would be impossible to put a hand to the Beekeeper without finding one's wrist in the monster's mouth.

They dismounted. The Beekeeper came right up to Molly—"Maeve, my heart's pulse!"—and hugged her for a long moment. Then she turned to Nemain, who took the Beekeeper's right hand and kissed it.

"Look at you, my heart, all grown, and quite the fine woman."

Nemain for once seemed not to know what to say. Finally, "This is my husband," she said, turning to Hob.

"Ah, yes, Sir Robert," said the old woman, taking Hob's hands in her own. How could she have known my name? he wondered, but it did not alarm him: her hands were warm and dry, and he found it a pleasant experience to have her hold to him like this. She did not let go immediately, but said as if in answer to his thoughts, "I have heard tales from my little birds, and seen things in my water mirror, and I welcome you all home, for this part of Erin will be the safer and the holier for your presence."

She released Hob at last, and turned to Jack. "And this is the formidable Jack Brown, a match for my young queen here." It was a moment before Hob realized that the "young queen" referred to was Molly herself; the Beekeeper was so ancient that even Molly was young to her. The old woman put a tiny hand to Jack's cheek, an intimate gesture that seemed perfectly natural. "You have had your troubles, too, child," she said to him; he grinned down at her, a little shyness in his manner.

The Beekeeper put a hand to the wolfhound's head. "And this is Conare. He is a great friend to me, but you must excuse him; he is not generally friendly with other people."

She turned to Molly. "You know that I do not often interfere in matters outside this valley, and that only when asked."

Molly did not hesitate. "'Tis your help I'm asking for now."

"This creature that *Banríon* Nathaira has created—I see it in the water mirror, and I think that this woman, this perverter of the Art, is like a stain in the world: she spreads her evil over everything; she dirties her own tribe; she fouls nature itself, until even the creatures in the grass are affected."

She put a hand on Hob's forearm. " 'Tis not that nature itself is kind," she said, as though he had made some objection. "It is not. But there is a difference between the cruelty some creatures find necessary to live, and cruelty for its own sake."

She turned back to Molly. "There are those of your people, Queen Maeve, whom she has taken, whose blood she has used to feed her sorceries. I have vowed not to leave this valley, but I was thinking that I must break that vow, for I could not let her continue her wickedness, and myself standing by. But now, you having returned at last, I see that 'twas not my place, but yours, to oppose her. I will help you in any way I may."

She looked about her as if trying to remember something. "First, I think, a bit of tea. Then I will give you a wasp." Hob was still trying to make sense of this when the Beekeeper turned and led the way into her cottage, trailed by Conare. The women followed; Jack looked at Hob and shrugged eloquently, and then went in, ducking to enter the low doorway. Hob stepped in after him and was immediately struck by the pleasant scent of the air, a mix of spices, cinnamon and clove and ginger and other things he could not identify.

The cottage was, as Molly had said, larger on the inside, for it ran back into what was essentially a long cave, against which had been built wattle-and-daub walls, with quilts and knitted blankets hung to the walls, keeping out the chill of the stone. This front room was itself longer than the outside cottage, and only the forepart had windows. There was a hearth with a small fire and a kettle swung out on an iron dog, and a round table with rush-seat chairs, and a small pantry, and the five skeletons, three on one side and two on the other, that sat in carved wooden chairs.

After his initial shock, which he thought he had concealed rather well, Hob stole a glance at the nearest skeleton. The bones were connected with leather thongs, each with a more elaborate knot than seemed necessary just to fasten one bone to another.

The Beekeeper was bustling around, and Nemain turned to Hob and said, very low, "Make no comment about . . ." and she nodded toward the chairs.

"Here, young man," she said to Jack, handing him the kettle. "Go out to yon stream and fill me this, not quite to the brim, mind you." Jack took the kettle and went out, as matter-of-fact as if he had been a scullion all his life.

In a little while they were all seated about the table, mugs of honey-sweetened tea before them, sweet cake, made with white flour and tasting strongly of ginger, on wooden plates. The giant Conare lay on the rug, curled right around the Beekeeper's chair. From time to time she would hold a hand down by her side, and the big head would come up, the jaws would open, showing an astounding hedge of wolf-killer teeth, and the Beekeeper would deposit a small wedge of ginger cake; at this point the shaggy gray hound would subside, thoughtfully mumbling the treat. Hob, after his initial amusement, realized that no one could come nigh the Beekeeper's chair without stepping on some part of Conare, and thus rousing the dragon.

Hob began to feel quite happy, almost a childlike, protected happiness; the very walls seemed to exude security. When he reached for another cake, though, and had first to move the hilt of his sword to a more comfortable position, suddenly he had to smile at the picture he presented to himself: the fierce Sir Robert having tea and cake in a cottage.

When they had finished and Jack was wistfully pursuing the last few crumbs around his plate, the Beekeeper said, "Let us leave the lads here, for I have something of the Art to give you." The women went outside, leaving the cottage door open, which pleased Hob, for he found that the skeletons, all of which seemed somehow to be looking at the table, and himself, and Jack, created a sinister contrast to the cozy interior of the cottage.

He turned in his seat. The women were out by the bee skeps, and the Woman of the Bees was placing a little straw box in Molly's hand, and then covering and wrapping it with a white linen cloth. There was a long conversation among the three women, Molly and Nemain obviously asking questions, the Beekeeper patiently answering.

Then it was done. Molly tucked the cloth-wrapped package away in her cloak, and Nemain came to the door and said, "We're away, lads; come say good-bye to Herself."

Another round of hugs and kisses, and encouragement from the Beekeeper—"You know what you must do, my dear"—to Molly, and they were up in the saddle and away, the Beekeeper standing and watching them go, a hand raised in farewell.

Up the sloping path, through the forest with its birdsong and its flowering trees, to the crest; a last look behind, and with a pang of loss they crossed the borderline of the Beekeeper's valley, and began the downward journey into the wide world of struggle and danger.

Chapter 25

When they were well down the mountainside, the track widening and the trees thinning, Hob spurred up close to Molly. "*Seanmháthair,* what were those skeletons the Beekeeper had sitting in chairs, and the chairs set back against her walls?"

Molly, swaying easily in her saddle, one hand beneath her cloak keeping secure the Beekeeper's gift, said, " 'Tis a long time I've known the Woman of the Bees, and when I was a younger woman and she teaching me, I went day after day, and one day the work keeping us with our heads down—'twas not the water mirror she was showing me this late afternoon, 'twas . . . I'm forgetting, but 'tis no matter, it kept us heedless of the hour, and it grew late, and she asked me to stay the night, and not to travel in the dark, and at some point she's telling me the story of the skeletons. There are two and three, you've noticed? Five in all."

"Aye," said Hob, "two on this side and three on the other."

"She's after telling me how she had two sets of enemies at different times in her life—two men in the one set, and a woman and two men in the other, and they did her harm, grievous harm—she gave no details, but it upset her to speak of it atall, and she not easily upset—and, any road, she overcame them."

Hob was beginning to see where this led, and he said, "The two are the two men, and the three are the woman and men? And she has kept their bones?"

Molly looked up at him, seated on great Iarann, and said, "Kept their bones, yes. And she's boiled them and cleaned the flesh from them, and prayed over them, and knotted them together with cunning knots—you saw the leather thongs, and the knots?"

Hob nodded. The road narrowed here to squeeze by a boulder, and he pulled the destrier to one side to let Molly and Nemain go past. Jack was trailing by a bit, and Hob did not wait for him, but kneed the big gray warhorse and filed through after the women. When he had caught up with Molly again, he prompted her: "The knots?"

"Aye, the knots; cunning, cunning knots, with her magic woven into them. And that night the Beekeeper bade me sit silent in a corner, and she composed verses listing the offenses of her enemies, and sang them to the skeletons, and myself sitting in the corner, and the back of my neck all a-tingle, and the skeletons arising one by one as she addressed them in song, and they creaking and knocking, and bending the knee with a grinding noise before her, and bowing and returning to their seats, one after the other. For she has not let them die the death but has retained their life force, trapped it within those bone cages, and they live on, reduced though they be."

"Holy Mary!" said Hob. "I can scarce credit it, it is so . . ."

"'Tis as we've told you, husband," said Nemain, riding on Molly's other side. "The world is stranger than your priests tell; and nowhere stranger than here, at the end of all land, and we forever looking at the ocean that rolls away to nowhere."

"Aye, or to Apple Island where British Arthur sleeps," said Molly. "Now when the Beekeeper had finished and the skeletons once more sat quiet in their chairs, she told me she did that each night, and that the verses were always different, though always on the same subject, the tale of their misdeeds, and her contempt for them, and each night they are forced to bow and kneel to her. She is in most things a fine and kindly woman, but having once seen this ceremony, I've never seen it again, and I hope never to do so. She made me a nice wee bed in a small room, and fed me well, but I slept but little that night, and ever since visit only in the daylight."

They rode in silence for some time. Then:

"You've seen the orchards, and the fields, and the bees?" said Molly.

"Aye," said Hob, pulling at Iarann's reins: a bird had

flown up from the grass beneath their feet, and the always aggressive destrier had snapped at it, making a real attempt to catch it. Destriers were trained to bite at opposing infantry, and this was a side effect.

"And how do you think a wee woman, so very old, does all that, day upon day?"

"Well, I . . ." Hob's voice trailed off as he considered this. In truth, he had not thought about it at all.

"On days when she has no visitors, she makes them get up from the chairs, and venture out upon the valley, and do what is needful: planting, pruning, tending the bees. She will not do it when others are visiting her, and 'tis something I myself have never seen, but she told me that and much more, and why would I doubt her, having seen what I've seen?"

Hob found that his mind was rebelling: here they were riding along in the sunlight—beneath him the solid gray bulk of his Norman destrier, in his nostrils the scents of leather and horse and the grass of Erin crushed beneath their mounts' hooves—and speaking of bone-men working in apple orchards. Then again, he thought, we are going to battle a centipede as big as a stable, and he could feel himself inwardly throwing up his hands in defeat, or perhaps acceptance—he had traversed the terrain of the known, and passed some kind of boundary-stone, and was now in the land of legend, of the tales told around the hearth on a winter's night.

He crossed himself and said a short prayer, and trusted to his adopted family's innate goodness, that the God he had been brought up with would not consider these unearthly practices some great sin. He knew what Monsignor da Panzano would have thought of it, but he thought that perhaps the young Berber priest, Father Ugwistan, who admired Molly so much, might have been more understanding. You know my heart, Sieur Jesus, he said within himself. You know my heart.

THEY WERE NOW COMING OUT onto the plain, and Molly prepared to increase their speed, for there was yet much of the day left, and she wanted to begin fashioning her weapon against the centipede, for who knew when that horrid beast would recover enough to resume its depredations? They were good riders, except for Jack, and he could keep up when needed. She kneed her mare and it sprang ahead, and Nemain began to pick up speed as well.

The giant Iarann had no trouble keeping pace with the smaller animals, even though Hob was clad in mail today to guard against any unwelcome meetings upon the trail, and soon they were riding full tilt westward, till they gained the approaches to Molly's home valley.

From the forested ridges mounted sentries that Molly had stationed to watch against enemies, human or otherwise, raised their short Irish spears in salute. Hob touched his helm to them as they passed, and soon they were riding through the gates, with more of Molly's kerns standing about, guarding the entryway, axes on their shoulders and javelins slung to their backs. With their voluminous cloaks drooping like wings, their long braided moustaches framing their mouths, they had an air of gloomy ferocity; they might have been a cluster of predatory birds.

But they saluted, and welcomed their queens with cheerful calls and whistles: "Grandmother! Little Mother!" Hob never failed to wonder at the informality of Irish clan life, compared with the strict protocol of Sir Jehan's or Sir Odinell's castle folk.

Then they were down in the grass of the bailey, the stable men taking their mounts away, and Molly issuing rapid orders: preparations needful for the night's work of spellcraft, materials to be assembled by the young women who assisted the queens at their Art, and to be brought to the workshop the women had set aside for such activities.

Nemain was all for beginning immediately, but Hob convinced her to rest a short while, and eat something, and Molly agreed. "Let us but sit a while and fortify ourselves, for the night will be long, and then tomorrow we must go forth against Nathaira's vile creation, for to wait a day might bring more death from that thing. At the same time, 'twould be foolish to fail tomorrow through weariness, or even to introduce a flaw tonight into the weapon we hope to forge."

Nemain fretted, but at last allowed herself to be convinced, when Hob quoted one of Molly's favorite proverbs: "'Tis not a delay for a reaper to stop and sharpen the scythe."

Chapter 26

Molly and Nemain had begun preparations for a long night of their secret practice of the Art, from which men were excluded. Tomorrow they would face the centipede, a daunting prospect, and Hob, to distract himself, had walked down with Daire and another tribesman named Rogan to a meadow surrounded by a sturdy log-and-post fence: here was one of the grassy fields maintained by the Ó Cearbhaills to graze their livestock. Hob had a bag of apples slung from his shoulder; the Irishmen were along to keep him company. In the center of the green expanse Milo was lying down, head up but drowsing. Hob dropped the sack at his feet and just leaned his forearms on the top rail.

The wind shifted, coming from behind the three men, and out in the field the ox suddenly turned his head and peered nearsightedly at the little group of men. He lumbered to his feet and came toward them, breaking into an inelegant half-trot, emitting the occasional short bleating call. He came right up to the fence and put his head over and snuffled at Hob's chest, and then gently butted his forehead against Hob, his blunted horns going wide of Hob's body. Hob embraced the huge neck, laughing, and stroked Milo's forehead, while the ox uttered groans of pleasure, some sort of ox language, his usual expression of deep contentment.

"Sure I'd heard you had an ox like a dog, Sir Robert, but I've never seen the like," said Daire, and Rogan put a hand out and stroked the side of Milo's broad neck.

Hob was not yet at ease enough before the two Ó Cearbhaill warriors to speak nonsense to the ox as he usually did; he contented himself with feeding him several apples, one of Milo's particular enthusiasms. From far across the meadow, Tapaigh and Mavourneen, noticing the group by the fence, were making their way toward them, and in due course they had their treats as well.

After a while Hob shouldered the bag again. "Well, gentlemen," he said, "on we go to the east pasture. I must pay my respects to my destrier, and then perhaps we may see if there's strong drink to be had at the hall—unless you'd prefer an apple or two?"

Behind the circle of Molly's rath the hill dropped sheer away to the next valley, the drop itself an effective wall. There near the edge of the slope, just inside the palisade of the rath, was a small outbuilding that Molly and Nemain used as a place of refuge and privacy to work their Art. No men were allowed within, and of women only those adept in the Art, or the young maidens of the clan who served as aides to their queens in these matters.

A steady stream of these girls, some of whom would go on to become practitioners of the Art, others who would not, but would remember this time in their lives with wonder, came and went from this little house of sorcery with demands from Nemain or Molly: bundles of hazel withes, lengths of leather thongs, neat's-foot oil, a small box of garnets from Nemain's bedchamber.

Hob and Jack, excluded, waited nearby, seated on benches in the grassy bailey, sharpening weapons, drinking a bit, bantering with the gateway guards. The afternoon wore on, slowly. At the evening meal, the two queens were absent; with the removal of the children to the shieling, the hall was unusually quiet; a glum mood prevailed.

Evening fell, and the clan by twos and threes went to their dwellings for the night. The young women and girls assisting Molly and Nemain were dismissed, but still the two queens worked on, the light of oil lamps and candles showing glimmers beneath the door and at the joins where the shutters did not close completely over the windows. Hob and Jack spread blankets on the grass in front of the workshop, and slept under the stars.

At dawn the men roused, and after a brief breakfast continued their vigil. Some of the young acolytes assembled by the door, in case they were needed, but none of the girls dared knock—who knew what delicate process they might interrupt?

Jack produced a pair of dice and the two men sat on the grass and threw dice without any enthusiasm. They were playing for straws, and Hob was losing: Jack had a little pile of fifteen or twenty straws in front of him.

The sun was halfway to its zenith when the door opened and Nemain, bleary-eyed, came out and sat down on the grass between Hob and Jack. She beckoned one of the girls and had her run to the kitchens; the girl returned with a wooden bowl of goat's milk, which she offered shyly to her young queen. Nemain thanked her in a voice low with fatigue, and the girl went back to her colleagues by the door.

"'Tis done, or mostly done—Herself is finishing the eyes."

Jack gave a glance of inquiry at Hob.

"The eyes?" said Hob.

"Och, aye; we're using the garnets."

Hob could see there was not much of use to learn from Nemain, so very tired was she. He settled in to wait patiently.

At last Molly appeared in the doorway. For all the difference in their ages, she seemed less fatigued than her granddaughter. All the same, she was subdued. "Nemain," she said, and went back inside. The young queen put a hand on Hob and a hand on Jack and heaved herself up to her feet. She disappeared within and a moment later the two women came out, carefully carrying between them a withy construction the size of an Irish wolfhound.

Hob and Jack got up and went over to it, wondering. It

was an image of—what? It had wings, but it was not a bird: it had too many legs. A dragon? Hob could not make it out; he could not make it out; he could—then he had it.

The long narrow head, the javelin-slim body: it was a wasp, the limbs of hazel withe knotted with leather thongs, the knots curiously similar to the ones the Beekeeper had used to assemble the skeletons of her enemies. The framework of the wings was hazel twig, but the wings themselves were gray silk; the eyes were clusters of garnets, fixed with some glue to the sides of the withy face. Between the back legs the abdomen terminated in a long, downcurving hollow reed, painted black.

Within the head itself was a small cage, and in that cage was a box, with wool, and embedded in the wool was the Beekeeper's gift: a wasp of the type the withy wasp represented, embedded in a small chunk of amber, perfectly preserved, the insect more jewellike than the garnets.

"'Tis the natural enemy of such as the centipede, and we will convince the centipede that 'tis real—it *will* be real, for a time—and it will do what it must do, according to its nature, though we will quicken the process, so that what takes time will happen almost at once," said Nemain.

He bent to peer at the amber tomb of the original wasp.

"'Twas drowned in that amber, very long ago; perhaps before there were men in Erin," said Molly. "Even, perhaps, before there were gods in Erin."

Hob looked at the construction. It was an elegant object, but it was like a statue of hazel withe, inert, and delicate, even fragile.

"It will kill that monster that we saw? That huge thing?" asked Hob. He did not wish to offend his beloved or her grandmother, but he could not keep the disbelief from his voice.

Molly spoke, quiet, weary: "Hob, my pulse, step in front of it."

He did as Molly asked; he looked at it. It was a withy statue of a wasp.

Molly spoke two words in antique Irish, too arcane for Hob to understand, and the creature stirred. The wings vibrated, they fluttered, and now Hob could see that they were of transparent stuff shot with dainty veins, and the wasp moved toward him, the red compound eyes seeming to fix on him with menace, with hunger.

The whole wolfhound-sized insect, with its armored yellow legs, its glossy black head and shoulders, and its hard red abdomen, coursed with vibrant life, and he snatched at his dagger, all thought swept away by a primitive terror, the hair prickling up on the back of his head, and Molly said something else, and there was a lifeless withy image before him, and himself hunched over in a tense-muscled defensive crouch. He straightened, slowly, feeling foolish. He slid the war dagger, the big iron-pommeled gift from Sir Balthasar, back in its sheath, and let out a long breath.

"I believe 'twill serve," he said in a voice that was not as steady as he would have liked.

CHAPTER 27

THEY CAME AGAIN TO THE DEstroyed village, Jack driving a wain with the hazel-withe wasp and a few barrels of other material, Daire and his picked squad of cavalry riding escort. Molly had the Irishmen wait a short distance away, out of sight over a hill, for she did not want them to distract her and her granddaughter at their conjuring, and also she feared their reaction to what would occur. Jack and Hob were under no such prohibition, and indeed were to help with the heavier work. The family's mounts, and the horses that had drawn the wain, were led away by Daire's men, for no horse would stand quietly near such a monster as the centipede.

Molly and Nemain set up the wasp facing the cliff, and Jack wrestled a tub of beef blood and offal to the edge of the rock and splashed it, part on the cliffside ground and part over the cliff edge, running down the rock.

For a time nothing happened. The waves broke with a muted roar, far below, and a small cloud of seagulls appeared, alighting to peck at the bits of beef, squabbling among themselves, hovering out a bit from the rock, suspended over the drop on their long narrow wings. The air filled with their piercing raucous cries; they maneuvered and landed and took flight again.

Molly and Nemain, who had not slept at all, kept up a low running chant, a song of summoning. The afternoon wore on. Suddenly the gulls, almost as one, leaped into the air and stood off from the cliff, hovering perhaps a score of yards out over the ocean, uttering cries of alarm. Under the circumstances, there could hardly have been a more sinister occurrence: something was coming.

The air filled with the spicy, not-quite-pleasant alien scent of the centipede, and the drumming footfalls were heard as it clawed its way up the rock. There was a moment when silence fell, and Hob and Jack looked at each other, wondering—could it have sensed its danger, and retreated? But they would have heard its retreating footsteps. What, then, was it doing? Hob often thought that one could tell what Sweetlove was thinking—"You're not Jack; where's my Jack?" and the like. But this monster—did thoughts form in that alien head?

Then some strange decision was reached, and the creature flowed with frightening speed up over the lip of the cliff and toward them, its thick sharp-pointed poison claws clacking together, its compound ocelli staring at them, its antennae questing.

At once Molly and Nemain began a full-throated chant, and the withy wasp vibrated, and before Hob's eyes was once again a real wasp, a giant emissary from the horror-haunted little world of the insects.

The centipede stopped its rippling advance toward them with that abruptness that characterizes insect movement. The wasp had fixed its attention on the centipede, and the centipede, for its part, had turned its head so that the ocelli on one side had the wasp in its view. For such an opaque and inhuman countenance, Hob thought, it did, with its targeting of the wasp, manage to convey dismay, even fear, although he was not sure if he had just imagined this.

The wasp stirred, quivered; a low vicious buzzing sound came from it and it lifted, it soared. At once the centipede's front segments came off the ground and it reared, reared, reaching for the wasp, now rising at a sharp angle, its wing-beats too rapid to see, and the centipede's poison claws closed sharply on air, just below the wasp. The wasp flew briskly out over the ocean, turned about and came in behind the centipede.

It landed squarely on the midmost segment of the creature; the long tube that trailed behind its abdomen now plunged into the monster's back. The centipede at first curled back upon itself, trying to reach its tormentor, but it could not quite bend that much. The wasp quivered, its abdomen pulsing, the tube pushing deeper and deeper into the centipede. There came an explosion of activity from the many legs, the repetitive segments, of the monster, and Molly's family retreated hastily. Clouds of dust and small stones were thrown into the air; the monster bucked and heaved, but the wasp clung and pumped poison and eggs into its flesh.

The thrashing slowed, as paralysis overtook the centipede, and at last it lay rigid, assuming a stonelike aspect, and the ocelli became glassy; the transparent membrane began to slide over the eyelike structure, but came up only halfway and stopped. The enormous beast lay utterly motionless.

Molly called out sharply, and the wasp pulled free its ovipositor and rose into the air. Once again it flew out over the ocean, curved about and flew back in over the immobile monster, to settle at Molly's feet. She reached in and removed the little box with the wool and the chunk of amber, within which was the preserved wasp body, and once again Hob was looking at a statue formed from hazel withe, motionless, almost flimsy.

He looked at the centipede. "Is it dead, then?"

Nemain said, "Well, no. The wasp paralyzes its victims, and lays its eggs, and the eggs hatch and the young feed on the victim's body."

"Merciful Christ!" said Hob. "And now we must wait for all that, and then we will have—more wasps?"

"Nay, we have oil and torches in the wain—we will burn it now, and so destroy it utterly."

"And will that destroy the eggs as well?" asked Hob, who could not but worry about a plague of wolfhound-sized wasps descending upon them.

"Hob," said Molly gently, "there are no eggs. 'Tis but a withy wasp. It has no eggs. It believed itself to have eggs, and it believed itself to have paralyzing poison, and the centipede believed it as well, and so 'tis paralyzed, and so it might as well have been true for them, but there are no eggs."

Hob looked at Jack. "The centipede believed . . . Well, let us get the oil, Jack. Let me face a Norse Gael with an ax—'tis almost soothing beside these horrors."

They went to the wain, and he vaulted up and rolled the barrel of poppy oil to the tailboard, and Jack muscled it down to the ground, and they rolled it over to the monster.

The body of the centipede proved combustible in itself, and with the aid of the oil, was reduced to ash in a remarkably short time. Molly took the withy wasp in one hand and walked to the wain and without ceremony tossed it in.

"There," she said, in a voice weary unto death, "sure, that's done. Tomorrow, we'll have to hunt that witch down, but we can do no more tonight. I'd not want to face her now, with her Crone power, and ourselves so tired."

Chapter 28

Exhausted, drained both physically and of that force which is the will to live life, to be interested and open to the world around, Molly and Nemain sat on a ledge of stone, slumped against one another. Molly's arm was wrapped tight about Nemain's shoulders.

Hob squatted before them, a cup in each hand. Jack poured *uisce beatha* from a jug into each cup, and Hob urged each woman to drink. He had never seen them so tired, not even after the long night's struggle with Sir Tarquin, years ago. Of course, he thought, the years themselves added weight to any difficulty; he looked at his wife, the dark circles that had come to rest beneath her eyes over these past weeks, the slack expression at the corners of her mouth, and he felt a tenderness welling up in him, strong and sweet, fueled by his concern for her.

Molly took a cup from him and drank, hardly seeming to know what she did, and when she'd finished she just held it till Jack sat beside her and gently took the empty vessel from her hand. Hob held the cup to Nemain's lips; she looked at him blankly over the rim. Then, as if just that moment grasping what he wanted her to do, sipped at the fiery stuff; sipped again.

She drew a deep breath. She looked around. "Where's my baby? Hob, where's my baby?"

"She's up at the shieling, treasure of my heart, with the other children. You know that, surely?"

"Oh," she said. She looked away inland, up the slopes toward the hills. "The shieling, yes."

Molly, though much older than Nemain, was strong as a bear. Already her voice was almost steady. " 'Tis safer for them now to be back at the hall. Hob, send someone to bring the children back."

"You go, Hob," said Nemain fretfully. "Go yourself, husband; bring me my baby." Her eyes were closing, opening, closing again; she was fighting to stay awake.

"I'll go," said Hob. "Rest, now; rest."

Nemain's eyes closed and she leaned against Molly, who was in turn braced against Jack. Jack was immovable as a boulder, and with one hand the dark man made a reassuring motion and then indicated that Hob should go.

Hob rose and went to where Daire stood near Iarann. He shed his mail hauberk and his gambeson and left them in the wain; it was a relief to be free of the weight and the heat. He tossed the reins back over the destrier's head and prepared to mount. Hob told Daire, "Have the women helped into the wain and escorted back to the rath; they are too weary to ride. You yourself pick five men and come with me. We're going to bring the children back, and an escort would not be amiss. I no longer trust peaceful appearances." Still, he did not expect real trouble, or he would have kept the mail on, heat or no heat.

They rode up the winding track the shepherds and goat-boys used to bring their charges up to the mountain grazing in spring and down to the valley in the fall. The track wound up and up, the slopes of the mountain covered with ling, a sea of tiny pale purple bells.

A turn around an outcrop led to a narrow defile, and from there they debouched into a bowl-shaped upland valley, protected from the winds by the ring of rock walls around it.

There was the shieling, a cluster of small stone huts for the shepherds, with a wood fence that enclosed a pen for the livestock at night, and the meadow for grazing, a brook winding through it. Sheep and goats dotted the meadow, with herd-boys among them.

Large gray shapes came streaming toward them from the nearest hut: wolfhounds. As they came near, the dogs recognized them, and what had begun as an attack turned into a leaping, away-and-back, running-in-circles greeting, all to the accompaniment of the deep harsh barking typical of the breed.

They came up to the shieling and dismounted, the dogs eddying about them, and now children ran out and added to the din. The guards Molly had assigned to the children stood back till some of the excitement had abated, then there were eager requests for news—how had it gone against the centipede, were any slain, and so forth. Damnat, the woman in charge of the children, came up to them.

"Greeting, Sir Robert, how fares it below?"

"Greeting, Mistress Damnat. I am glad to say that we have prevailed: the dragon-beast is dead. You may get the children ready and into the wains; Daire here will escort you down. But I will carry Macha Redmane down with me now. Her mother is weary from the battle; she is fretful; I think seeing the child will soothe her."

For a long moment Damnat said nothing, and Hob felt a hand begin to close on his heart.

"*Banríon* Nemain, she, she, brought the child away, a little while since—did she not tell you, Sir Robert?"

They were looking at each other, with mirrored expressions of sick surprise. Both knew what had happened; each hoped the other would say something that would offer an innocent explanation.

Hob said, in a flat dead voice, "My lady wife sent me here direct, to collect the child."

"Oh, but, but, then—" She stumbled to a halt. " 'Twas *Banríon* Nemain, *'twas*! Her face, her voice, her walk—by She Whom I swear by, I did not know, I could not—"

"Hush, hush. That demon has put on her aspect; you cannot be blamed for it, woman—they have powers, and we are as children before them." He turned to Daire. "That hag"—*cailleach* was the word he used—"has her."

The Irishman nodded once. His face had paled, and the freckles stood forth on his forehead, and he twisted one of his two braids—it had a crow-skull weight on the end, the hair threaded through the eye sockets and tied off, and now he was turning the bone around and around, unconscious of what he did, blue eyes far away, a growing horror seeping into his expression.

Hob put a hand on his shoulder to bring him back. "Daire—you know this land from your childhood." The kern had been in exile for years, but all his life before that had been lived here.

"Och, aye?" Daire looked as if he knew what Hob would say and yet hoped he would not say it.

"Bring me to her cave," said Hob. It was not a request.

Daire nodded; he walked around his horse and mounted, and turned it without another word: a man riding to the gallows.

Hob mounted Iarann. To Damnat he said, "Find the fastest rider here and send him to my lady wife; tell her and her grandmother as well that I've gone to *Banríon* Nathaira's cave, that she has Macha Redmane, and to come there with all haste. With the other riders and guards, get the children into the wains and down to the rath: this place is no longer safe from that witch."

He turned the massive gray head about, and by the pressure of his knees, told Iarann what he wanted: the destrier bunched his hindquarters and leaped into a gallop. Daire gave a shout to his rouncey and they shot off after Hob's receding back. Once through the defile and back on the sheep track he passed Hob. Halfway down the mountain he veered off into a meadow, heading north, heading toward the Cave of Cats, Nathaira's lair: the mouth of Hell.

Chapter 29

Daire pulled up at the foot of the hill. The clifftop road Hob and Daire were on had a drop to the ocean on his left; in front Nathaira's cliff rose further still, climbing toward the sky. A low hill, an apron of dusty soil, seeded with rocks small and large—a plowman's nightmare—ran up to the cave mouth. The front of the cliff plunged into the Western Ocean. Here on its southern side the cave opening showed as a semicircle of ink against the sheer sandstone wall.

They rode up the slight slope to the cliff face. The cave entrance showed nothing; the shadow within was intensely black. It looked like a natural cave—it might have been a bear's den, or a den of wolves—but for the crude wood fence that marked off a patch of land in front. A simple gate, with a simple latch, gave access.

He and Daire dismounted. Daire took Iarann's reins from Hob and stood pulling at his drooping moustaches.

"Can ye not wait for the women, Sir Robert? For 'tis fey work, and 'tisna the province of menfolk, and your sword will be of no more use than a twig of heather, and—'Tis that I'm Queen Maeve's man, you ken, but, but, I darena . . ." He was twisting the reins of both horses about his knuckles; he was breathing heavily, and a sheen of sweat glistened upon his forehead.

Hob looked at him. "There is no shame to you in this. But my daughter is in there, and I am going to enter in to her and, Jesus aid me, to bring her out. Stay you here, friend Daire, and tell my lady wife and her grandmother where I've gone, and that Redmane is within, taken by that witch of perdition, and tell them to come aid me, or to come avenge me."

He loosened his sword in its scabbard, and strode up to the gate. It seemed to be a simple enclosure, as one that a cottage would put about its vegetable garden, yet he feared a trap, and could not tell if he sensed a dire energy to it, or if he but imagined it. He hesitated a moment, then shook his head angrily and reached out his gauntlet and lifted the latch. It moved easily, and he stepped through. Nothing happened. He left it open, and walked into the cave entrance, so like a gaping mouth, hungry, menacing.

He passed into darkness, but after a moment his eyes adjusted, and the daylight outside, diffused though it was, gave a wan illumination to the passage. He went forward, and a bend in the rock effectively cut off all help from the sun.

He was now in a short narrow tunnel, perhaps ten feet

in length, spurs of the rough-hewn stone projecting now from the walls, now from the ceiling, so that he had to duck or swerve as he went. This section was unlit, but the room beyond had torches fixed in the walls, and enough light spilled out into the entrance passage to enable him to avoid the obstacles.

He emerged into a room perhaps a third the size of Blanchefontaine's hall, a handful of torches in sconces fixed to the rough stone walls, the ceilings soaring into shadow where the torchlight could not reach, the floor seething with cats.

There must have been a hundred of them: they curled up on woven-grass mats; they drank from stone bowls; they rubbed against the rock walls; they mated in the dark recesses. Over all was the pungent eye-watering ammoniac smell of cat urine.

Gradually they became aware of him. One by one they turned and sat facing him, ears flattened, fangs glinting in the torchlight: they gave every evidence of hostility, and he put a hand to his sword hilt. He wondered if they were only cats, or something more; he felt as though a cold hand had been placed upon his spine. He had a strange reluctance to draw his sword, as though that might precipitate an attack, or the sound alert the Crone.

He put a foot into the space between two of the cats, and took a step, and then another, the cats shifting in place so that he was always the cynosure of a ring of cats, their countenances somehow conveying a more-than-animal expression of personal hatred. But he kept moving: somewhere ahead was his daughter, and nothing would interrupt his progress, if he had to hack his way through a thousand cats.

At last he was through the main group of animals. At the far side of the chamber was another round entryway, another short dark tunnel. He passed through, moving more and more warily, and entered a smallish room, and stopped short.

Torches here lit a waist-high block of stone, as long as a tall man, and perhaps a yard wide, the surface sunk a few inches, so that there was left a raised border all around. Grooves cut in the stone ran from every corner and from the sides to a central basin-shaped depression. Hob stared at it; the altar, if that was what it was, gave off a dark radiance; it almost shouted its purpose. It was so fashioned that a bleeding body lying upon it would fill the central basin, the blood coursing down the channels, with no least drop lost over the side. Hob could see it so vividly that for a moment he stood as one stunned.

There was a movement in the shadows at the far side of the chamber. Now he saw Nathaira coming into the torchlight, her black hair wildly tangled, her gray eyes, underlined with dark semicircles, fixed on his face with a savage pleasure. Her face was harshly handsome; her shift left bare her arms, knotted with long low woman's muscle; her sinewy hands moved over one another in a washing motion. On every finger of her right hand were what looked to be brass thimbles. He looked more closely—they ended in curved needle-sharp claws. She took a stone dish from a recess in the wall and placed it at the head of the stone table, and it made a small *clink,* and he saw that it was filled with an amber liquid, and a little curl of bitter smoke drifted on the surface. As he watched, she dipped half the length of the brazen claws in the sinister brew. Mary Mother, he thought, has she found some way to milk that centipede of its venom?

There were cats here and there in this room as well, though never so many as in the antechamber. A cat leaped up on the stone table and licked delicately at one of the grooves.

"Robert the Englishman," she murmured in a rasping contralto. "Is it that you're a wise man, or is it that you're a fortunate man, you coming in as you are, and you empty-handed? Had you entered with a drawn weapon, the guardian spells I left would have torn you like a rabbit among wolves."

She pointed to a stone bench along the wall. "Sit! Be my guest this night! You are here in good time to see me feed your daughter's heart to my little ones, to see me bathe my brow in her blood."

And now he looked beyond her, into the dim alcove from which she had emerged—there was Macha Redmane, her small hands grasping the bars of a wicker cage, just big enough for her to stand erect. Her eyes were fixed on him.

"Macha," he croaked.

She turned toward Nathaira. "My father has come here to kill you. I told you he would, but you would not listen."

The Crone looked at her with a flat hostile countenance: the look a snake might direct at a bird within its striking distance. Then she turned back to Hob, and began to sing.

Hob understood at once that he had waited too long

to act. The song she sang, in the Gaelic of the Scots, in the dialect of the Western Isles, was beyond his ability to decipher, even with his knowledge of Irish, but its effects were unmistakable. The rough-edged contralto seemed to echo in the hollows of his bones; a sudden weakness seized his limbs and a dull ache began at the backs of his hands, his wrists. It was like falling ill between one breath and another, or aging half a lifetime in a moment.

His daughter said something about a cat, but sound was receding, swamped beneath the roaring in his ears. His vision seemed to fade at the edges of the room. He bit his lip; the pain brought him back to himself, and he said within himself, *I am Robert the Englishman, I am Robert the Englishman, I have come to kill you, I am*—and then who he was was drowned in the roaring, the gray ice, the gray eyes with the fan of fine lines radiating from their corners, the blackness that swept in from the corners of his eyes. Her black hair blew across his eyes, her song rang in his ears; he could no longer see the cage in the corner, he could barely hear his daughter's voice. Cat, she said, or he thought she said.

Roaring in his ears, his hand leaning on the stone altar, his legs feeling like stone; the Crone rasped and hissed her song, the hiss mixing with the roar and somehow chilling his limbs; he leaned against her will as though against the winter wind. He thought he heard a child's voice, so faint, so faint—it was Redmane's voice, and she said—no, he must have fallen partway, because he was clinging to the lip of the table.

He heaved himself upright in a panic and took a step,

moving his leg from the hip because his knee would not bend, and then another step but more slowly, and then he could not take the next step. He could feel the ice creep up his legs, stiffening them, he could hear nothing but a hiss and a roar, he could see nothing but Nathaira's gray eyes, boring into him from under her handsome crow-dark brows.

He felt tears on his cheek, but could not spare a moment to wipe them away. Nathaira seemed to be obscured by a red mist; he blinked feverishly, and the sorceress grew clear, but a moment later she was hazed in red again, and the warm tears fell and fell on his cheeks. Robert the Englishman: his eyes were filling with blood.

Was his daughter calling to him? He was not sure—it might have been the witch queen: Their voices were very similar, were they not? Something warm and liquid ran from his ears and down his neck. Cat, said Nathaira or Redmane. He was down at the foot of the table, and the Crone was at the head, and he had been here for a very long time, watching her dusk-gray eyes, watching her raise her clawed hand toward him, flexing the fingers that dripped amber liquid upon the table. Where the drops struck they smoked upon the stone. She was killing him where he stood; yet should he reach her where she stood, she would claw poison into his flesh.

Something concerning a cat, he thought. One or the other was saying it, and he thought it was an interesting question, to determine who it was; it might pass the time while he waited here, so far down the long, long stone table that was a blood-grooved altar, waiting for the ice to reach his heart and lock it shut between one beat and the next.

"Cat," said his daughter again, or was there an echo from the cave's crude stone walls, or was there an echo in his mind? No, Nathaira had said it, surely, or had sung it. She *was* a handsome woman, her eyes, with their delicate crow's-feet, gray as evening, her hair black as night, and her low pleasant rasp of a voice singing, singing in his blood-drenched ears.

"Cat," said his daughter, and he thought that, that she, he closed his eyes and he thought that she . . .

"Cat!" said Redmane, and holding to the table with his right hand and barely awake and without a thought in the stunned silence of his mind he swept out his hard left hand and scooped the cat up and tossed it underhand at Nathaira's handsome face.

The cat landed in a whirl of limbs, partly on the Crone's head and partly on her shoulder, struggling for balance and purchase. A flailing paw caught the witch queen's eye, scratching it closed, and Nathaira gave a loud cry and batted at the animal with her brass-nailed right hand, her other clapped over the wounded eye, her Crone strength sending the animal tumbling across the little room, the cat dead from the poison before it hit the cave wall.

Nathaira stared, one-eyed, appalled: she had broken her *geis.*

Hob felt the cessation of pressure. His blood running hot once again, his legs obeying him, his breath sweeping into opened lungs, Robert the Englishman began to come around the altar-table, gathering speed, Hob moving freely again, Sir Robert sweeping his sword out smoothly from its scabbard, the blade a gold gleam in the torchlight. And now Nathaira made an attempt to rally, her right hand drawn back, the fingers curled, the amber poison coating half the brazen nail-guards and dripping from the tips, but Robert the Englishman, in a red vengeful fury, his sword coming back from the drawing-out in a curl of golden light, struck her hand off at the wrist, smoothly altered the direction of his blade, and swept her head from her shoulders, her body dropping straight down like a puppet from the morality plays and her head rolling across the rock floor to fetch up against the wall, upright, staring at him. For a terrible moment he thought her head lived, so directly did she look at him with eyes wide, but then he moved to the side and her eyes did not follow.

A cat came in; it was a cat, but he thought it might also be more than a cat, and he watched it narrowly. It settled by Nathaira's body and began to lap at the blood from her neck.

He sheathed the sword and strode briskly to the cage. "Step back, sweeting," he said, and when Macha backed up he put a heavy foot through the wicker of the cage side. He pulled loose the fragments and she ducked through the hole and then he had her up in his arms, hugging her and kissing her cheek, her eye, her temple. Yet he kept watch on the cat: in this terrible place, one could not slack one's vigilance.

"I tried to warn her," said Redmane in a small voice. She put her face into his neck, her eyes shut tight. "I told her you were coming and that you would kill her if she did not let me go, but she thought I was just trying to frighten her, and she laughed."

"Let us go out into the air," he said, and he walked carefully back through the rooms. The cats in the outer room looked at him as he passed, but already they seemed less focused, less demonic, more catlike.

They came outside, and the breezes from the Western Ocean cooled his face; gulls drifted up over the cliff walls, crying one to another; the sea air washed him clean of the scent of cat. But he did not stop till he had passed through the little garden gate in the fence around the foreyard of Nathaira's cave. It seemed a symbolic boundary, and he knew from Molly and Nemain that a symbol in the hands of a mage is as much a weapon as an ax in the hands of a gallowglass.

Just outside the gate, Daire stood, still holding the two horses. Hob stepped through the gate, and Daire went to one knee. He regarded Hob with a kind of awe mixed with a little fear: Who was this man who went into a demon's lair and came out unscathed? The Irishman stood again, and now Hob could see that his face streamed with tears. Hob himself felt that he could not speak just then. He patted Daire's shoulder as he passed, and carried Redmane over to a wide boulder near the cliff edge, and sat, the child still clinging to his neck, and looked out over the ocean, and was quiet for a time. Daire hung back, leaving the two to themselves: a man of delicate instincts.

Then Daire's horse whickered. Someone was coming.

Chapter 30

A TROOP OF RIDERS, LOOSELY STRUNG out along the trail, was coming full tilt toward the cave, the horses lathered and panting, toiling up the slope. Behind the two lead riders, a length or two ahead of the pack, floated long banners of silver hair, red hair: Molly and Nemain. After them could now be discerned a score of Irish riders, and toward the back, Jack galloping along with them, sitting a sturdy horse in his graceless style.

"Mommy is coming," he told Macha Redmane, and the child lifted her head and looked down along the trail.

They thundered up, Molly and Nemain flinging themselves off and the other riders slowing, the horses milling in a rough circle, winding down to a halt. Fergus dropped off his horse and caught the reins of the two queens' mounts.

Nemain ran to them and snatched Redmane up and crushed her into a hug, burying her face in the child's hair, her eyes shut tight, her body taut as a drumhead. Molly rapidly ascertained that Macha was unharmed, then strode to her horse and ripped a hazel staff from a loop on her saddle. She started toward the cave, her face the mask of a lioness, an expression of implacable ferocity.

"She is quite dead, Grandmother," said Hob.

Molly halted at the gate, but did not look at Hob.

"I would look upon her," she said, and started forward again. She disappeared into the cave. Moments passed, and she emerged slowly and walked back through the gate, and carefully closed and latched it, and came over to Hob. She held to the staff with one hand, bent to him, and turned his face toward her with her other hand. She kissed one eye, then the other, and then his forehead. Then she straightened and went to Nemain, kissed the child, and kissed Nemain as well.

Behind him Hob could hear Daire murmuring, recounting to Fergus and his squad what he knew of what had happened. A heavy hand fell upon Hob's shoulder, thumped him gently. He looked up: Jack, beaming at him.

Molly went near the cliff and looked out over the Western Ocean. She began to sing: not a chant, a real song, but without words, just pure tones, and Nemain went to her, Redmane on her hip, and joined in, a soaring melody sweeping up and up, graceful as the wheeling gulls, an arc of purest beauty.

If ever I've heard a hymn, thought Hob, Jesus be my savior, this is a hymn. He looked in wonder at his daughter, his wife, her grandmother who now was also his liege: Who were these fey women, their names now inextricably tangled in the roots of his heart?

AFTER A TIME they came to him where he sat, and Nemain put Macha Redmane on his lap, and sat beside him, and put her arm about his waist. Molly sat to his other side, and Jack sat down beside her. Behind them, the Irishmen squatted, silent, respectful, reins wrapped about their fists.

"I must ask, child," said Molly. "How is it that you were able to slay that witch, and she a woman of so great power that Nemain and myself were dreading to face her? For I would have said that she would have killed you for certain."

"She nearly did so," said Hob quietly. "But my daughter is of your blood and of Nemain's blood. I have not the second sight, and I know little of these matters of Art, but you yourself have said it: I have an eye in my head, and I tell you I think she is to be one of the great adepts. Through the storm of sorcery that witch queen drove at me, Macha Redmane made her voice heard, and guided me, and told me what to do, and myself dying on my feet—I felt it, I felt myself dying!—yet she told me, or told my body, for as near as I can recall, I was far into my last sleep, not completely, but far in, and she said one word—or I could hear but the one word—and *she made me know what it meant!* How, I know not. I care not. We live, and Nathaira is dead."

He kissed the top of the little head before him. His family was all about him, and they had come to home and safety at last, and he sat and breathed salt air and was filled with a blunt slow surge of unutterable joy.

Nemain and Hob and Molly and Jack: they were all facing the lip of the cliff, perhaps ten feet away. Beyond was the drop to the tremendous expanse of the Western Ocean, slow massive swells rolling in from far out at the end of the eye's ability, crashing in foam and thunder far below, battering ancient Erin's coast.

Hob had one arm about his daughter, and now he put his free hand onto Nemain's thigh, palm up, and she put her hand on it and interlaced her fingers with his, and so they sat, silent. Peace, and joy, and no sound but the boom of the waves far below, the whistle of the air off the ocean. The sea wind came in bursts, lifting the women's hair in floating wings behind them, and Macha's flame hair blew back into his face, blinding him with a red veil, so that though the view before them swept out through a gulf of gray air to the line that marked the edge of the world, his daughter filled all his sight, his daughter was all he could see.

Glossary of Irish Terms

a chuisle	pulse, heartbeat [uh KOOSH-la] (direct address; literally: "O pulse")
a Dheaidí	Daddy [uh YAD-dy] (direct address)
annlann	condiment, flavoring [ON-lun]
arracht	monster [are-OCHT]; (plural: arrachtaigh) [are-OCH-thee]
a rún	love, dear [uh ROON]
Banríon Maeve abú	Queen Maeve forever!
Bean na beacha	Woman of the Bees [BAN neh BACH-a]

cailleach	hag *or* witch (as Hob is using it; can also just mean "old woman" when combined with a good adjective to make it a positive term: compare *cailleach feasa*, "wise old woman, "fortune-teller") [KYLE-yuch] ["ch" as in "loch"]
cláirseach	Irish harp [KLAUR-shock]
eisléine	grave garment; what the dead are buried in [ESH-LAY-inuh]
Gall-Ghaedheil	the Norse Gaels [GOWL-GHAYLE]
gallóglaigh	[gal-OH-gluh or gal-OH-glig]
geis	a supernatural command or obligation to perform a certain action, or a taboo that forbids a certain action [GESH]
Innse Gall	the Hebrides (literally "Islands of the Foreigners," i.e., the Norse) [EEN-shuh GOWLE]
léine	the smock-like shirt that is the basic Irish garment [LAY-inuh]
Mavourneen	my sweetheart (Irish *mo mhuirnín*) [muh VOOR-nyeen]

ochone	an exclamation of sorrow; woe (Irish *ochón*) [och-OWN]
ríastrad	distortion, warping [REES-thrud]
seanmháthair	grandmother (literally: "old mother") [shan-VAW-her]
sin-seanmháthair	great-grandmother [shin-shan-VAW-er]
spalpeen	rascal, layabout (Irish *spailpín*, itinerant laborer) [SPAL-peen]
stór mo chroí	treasure of my heart [STORE muh KREE]
Treibheanna na Gaillimhe	Tribes of Galway: the fourteen great trading families of Galway [TRAY-vennuh naw GAL-ivuh]
Uí Bháis	Tribe of Death (literally "Descendants of Death" or "Grandsons of Death") [EE VAWSH]
uisce beatha	whiskey (literally: "water of life") [ISH-kuh BAHA]

Glossary of Archaisms and Dialect Terms

culver	dove (term of endearment)
men of their hands	men proficient with weapons
mort	a great deal, a great many (lit. "death"; a mortal amount)
sennight	a week (seven-night)
sylvester	a wild man, one who lives at an animal level in the forest, drawing strength from nature. A figure in myth stretching back through the Green Man of medieval legend to Enkidu in *The Epic of Gilgamesh*.
tarse	medieval slang for "penis"
wodewose	a wild man of the forest; a sylvester

About the Author

Douglas Nicholas was an award-winning poet whose work appeared in numerous publications, among them *Atlanta Review, Southern Poetry Review, Sonora Review, Circumference, A Different Drummer,* and *Cumberland Review,* as well as the *South Coast Poetry Journal,* where he won a prize in that publication's Fifth Annual Poetry Contest. Other awards included Honorable Mention in the Robinson Jeffers Tor House Foundation 2003 Prize for Poetry Awards, second place in the 2002 Allen Ginsberg Poetry Awards from PCCC, International Merit Award in *Atlanta Review*'s Poetry 2002 competition, finalist in the 1996 Emily Dickinson Award in Poetry competition, honorable mention in the 1992 Scottish International Open Poetry Competition, first prize in the journal *Lake Effect*'s Sixth Annual Poetry Contest, first prize in poetry in the 1990 Roberts Writing Awards, and finalist in the Roberts short fiction division. He was also recipient of an award in the 1990 International

Poetry Contest sponsored by the Arvon Foundation in Lancashire, England, and a Cecil B. Hackney Literary Award for poetry from Birmingham-Southern College. He is the author of *Something Red* and its sequels, *The Wicked* and *Throne of Darkness,* fantasy novels set in the thirteenth century, as well as *Iron Rose*, a collection of poems inspired by and set in New York City; *The Old Language,* reflections on the company of animals; *The Rescue Artist,* poems about his wife and their long marriage; and *In the Long-Cold Forges of the Earth*, a wide-ranging collection of poems. He is survived by his wife, Theresa, and Yorkshire terrier, Tristan.

Interior Images

PAGE 1: *Ionian Dancing Girl* by John William Godward

PAGE 129: *Clytemnestra After the Murder* by John Collier

PAGE 217: *The Magic Circle* by John William Waterhouse

Printed in the United States
By Bookmasters